PAI 2015

Renegades of perdition

Paine. Lauran.

CARVER COUNTY LIBRARY

Renegades of
Perdition Range

OTHER FIVE STAR WESTERN
TITLES BY LAURAN PAINE:

Tears of the Heart (1995); *Lockwood* (1996); *The White Bird* (1997); *The Grand Ones of San Ildefonso* (1997); *Cache Cañon* (1998); *The Killer Gun* (1998); *The Mustangers* (1999); *The Running Iron* (2000); *The Dark Trail* (2001); *Guns in the Desert* (2002); *Gathering Storm* (2003); *Night of the Comancheros* (2003); *Rain Valley* (2004); *Guns in Oregon* (2004); *Holding the Ace Card* (2005); *Feud on the Mesa* (2005); *Gunman* (2006); *The Plains of Laramie* (2006); *Halfmoon Ranch* (2007); *Man from Durango* (2007); *The Quiet Gun* (2008); *Patterson* (2008); *Hurd's Crossing* (2008); *Rangers of El Paso* (2009); *Sheriff of Hangtown* (2009); *Gunman's Moon* (2009); *Promise of Revenge* (2010); *Kansas Kid* (2010); *Guns of Thunder* (2010); *Iron Marshal* (2011); *Prairie Town* (2011); *The Last Gun* (2011); *Man Behind the Gun* (2012); *Lightning Strike* (2012); *The Drifter* (2012); *The Texan Rides Alone* (2013); *The Story of Buckhorn* (2013); *Shadow of a Hang Rope* (2014)

RENEGADES OF PERDITION RANGE

A WESTERN STORY

LAURAN PAINE

FIVE STAR

A part of Gale, Cengage Learning

GALE
CENGAGE Learning·

Farmington Hills, Mich • San Francisco • New York • Waterville, Maine
Meriden, Conn • Mason, Ohio • Chicago

Copyright © 2014 by Lauran Paine, Jr.
Five Star™ Publishing, a part of Cengage Learning, Inc.

LIBRARY OF CONGRESS CATALOGING-IN-PUBLICATION DATA

Paine, Lauran.
    Renegades of perdition range : a Western story / Lauran
Paine. — First edition.
        pages ; cm
    ISBN 978-1-4328-2849-3 (hardcover) — ISBN 1-4328-2849-5
(hardcover)
    I. Title.
PS3566.A34R46 2015
813'.54—dc23   2014038496

First Edition. First Printing: March 2015.
Published in conjunction with Golden West Literary Agency.
Find us on Facebook– https://www.facebook.com/FiveStarCengage
Visit our website– http://www.gale.cengage.com/fivestar/
Contact Five Star™ Publishing at FiveStar@cengage.com

Renegades of
Perdition Range

CHAPTER ONE

He reached a flat stretch and roweled his horse over into a long lope. Nighttime cold pushed against him and brittle stars spread their milky ferment through the curving black heavens overhead. He had left the flat country behind now. There was this bony spine to cross again with Arizona Territory all around him in the night.

He knew his way, which was a great help because, even if there'd been a moon to guide him, there were still very few landmarks in this huge flow of empty land. Many a man had perished here, and not entirely from the bullets of snake-eyed watching Apaches, either.

There was no water for forty miles, until he got to Tucson and Little Eye Spring, except for a secret place he knew of in a jumble of huge boulders. Not more than a handful of others knew about that secret place, and those others were Apaches, every man jack of them. They'd be about as likely to tell a stranger where to find water as they'd be likely to welcome him into that empty wasteland between where he now was and where he was going, anyone at all, white skin or red skin.

He got high up eventually, and had the feeling that the entire world tilted from east to west. The weight of those bald, sere, and melancholy hills pressed in around him. Once, a cougar screamed and his horse shivered, but that old cat was a long way off and the rider could smile a little. There wasn't much worth stalking in this desert world except lizards and horned toads, rabbits and the like. Not enough to keep a big cat from getting pleats in his belly. The old cougar wouldn't stay long. He'd head east into the Dos Cabezas, some place like that anyway, where there were trees and bigger game. The only hunters who could survive here were rattlesnakes and men, but even for them it was a touch-and-go proposition. Mostly, when movement was sighted, it was someone passing through, like now. Perhaps not in the night, but if a rider had good enough reason, the night was the best time. He'd leave tracks. There was no way to avoid that, even during the rainy season, because no one ever knew when rain would come on the desert. But there was something just as good as rain for obliterating tracks—wind.

This whole hushed and empty world was subject to big blows. Initially the Mexicans had called those winds Santa Anas, meaning they stirred up huge clouds of dust such as that which with the great armies of Mexico's old time *Generalissimo* Antonio Lopez de Santa Anna had filled the heavens, but that had been a long time ago and now people just called the winds Santa Anas without knowing, or caring where that name had come from. Even the Indians called the winds Santa Anas.

Still, like the rain, one never knew when a Santa Ana would come. Certainly the rider cresting the top out of those gaunt old hills didn't know. The only thing he was certain of was that nighttime was an ally. He used it as one, too, breaking downward from the chilly heights upon an ancient trail worn deep into lava rock, letting his horse pick the way and the gait because up here there was treacherous footing.

He was two hours from the rearward trail when he felt the peaks on either side hunching their shoulders for the last time before the trail leveled off and the huge expanse of dreary plain began again. Creekbeds ran down those barren slopes that, if there had been more earth and less lava rock, might have been great gashes deeply cut by storms, but that showed now in the eerie night only as pale, leached trail ways for run-offs. To a rider familiar enough with this frighteningly big and silent land, those pale traces were a sign that he was heading north, and this far at least was the way he wanted to go.

Once back down upon flat country again, he swung almost due west, pushed his horse over into another easy lope, and rode along like that for nearly three miles before he reined down, halted, dismounted, and stood for almost ten full minutes, just listening. Acoustics here were excellent almost any time, but in the night they were particularly good. Still, he heard nothing, not even the wail of coyotes, so he stepped back up over leather and went onward again, slower this time, slower and more relaxed.

He was still a long way from his destination, but as long as nothing interfered he'd make it in good shape. Every time a rider crossed this country, though, he was gambling. A snake-bit horse, for example, could put a man afoot so far from succor he couldn't possibly hope to survive. In other places, the Dos Cabezas for instance, he could gather twigs, light a big fire, and wait. Sooner or later someone would come to investigate. But out here there was nothing from which to make a signal fire. And water was the mainstay of life, more so here than other places. Even in the springtime, like now, temperatures soared upon the daytime desert, sweat dried upon a man's skin before it ever touched his shirt. The Apaches said they could live two, sometimes three, days without water here. They also said, and it was true, a white man couldn't live more than two days, and even then he'd have to be an exceptional white man.

In the old days Mexicans called this desert crossing *jornada del muerto*—Journey of the Dead One. They had plenty of reason for calling it that, too, for more Mexicans had perished in this limitless land than Indians, or settlers, either, for that matter;

more Mexicans had died here than all the combined fatalities of the other two groups combined. So many in fact that Mexico had given up her early-day colonization schemes, left the land to Apaches, and it had remained their stronghold and heartland until not too long before now. Although there were still a few dissidents in the secret places, mostly the Apaches had become cowboys for the desert cow outfits, teamsters, wild-horse runners, laborers, or just plain settlement loafers, something at which they were by heritage very accomplished. Scarcely a town anywhere around didn't have a few dozen expressionless, short, and sturdy Apache loafers living upon its outskirts. Sometimes the men worked long enough to buy something, a new carbine, a pair of boots, a bolt of bright cloth, but not many kept at it. Thousands of years of being ferocious marauders and incredibly adept thieves could not be overcome so quickly. Anyway, the new rulers of this lost world weren't sufficiently interested to try and change them; it required all the toughness and ingenuity settlers had to make this land give them a living. They had no time, nor inclination, to take on any other job than the elemental one of survival.

All it took to break the hearts of those desert cowmen was one dry spring or one depressed cattle market. It was often asked why anyone, unless he was hiding from the law, would willingly bury himself in this empty, endless world. And the answer was not a simple one. Partly it was because, like that rider passing across the desert in the night, somewhere in every man there was a compelling urge to live an uncomplicated life, to ride free and sit tall in the saddle. Partly, too, it was because here, in this lawless waste, a man was just as strong, just as sound, just as good as he could prove himself to be. Or just as ornery and worthless.

Because this was so, when one encountered the cowmen in this quiet world, one came upon individualists. No two were the same, not even in their determination to survive. The present rider, for example, was as wrung-out as a man could be. He was tall and lean and easy-moving. He rode with grace and also with a certain degree of wildness to him. His eyes constantly moved, his ears listened, his muscles were bunched and easy at the same time. He was, in his own way, as coiled as a spring and as slouched as an old rag. What he was not, although at first glance he seemed to be, was indifferent or careless.

He proceeded down at a slow pace that breathless night, relaxed now, feeling no longer the quick tingle of excitement, his reins looped and his fingers running gently through the cool, crisp contents of his saddlebags. The night was on his side, and so was the desert with its nakedness closed out by motionless gloom. He made a smoke, deeply inhaled, exhaled, closed the saddlebags, and slouched along, taking the pulse of the world around him, thinking his private thoughts, considering how deceptive life could be sometimes, how mild and benign up to a point. This spring, for instance, it had come with benevolent warm rains to fetch up the grass, to brighten lichen on the mountain sides, to bring golden days of freshness and good warmth. He had sat his horse, watching those clean, high-flying wedges of geese go past, northbound. He had laughed with the others when the Connells made their gather. He had waved as the Connells had pushed on toward Tucson with the first cattle drive of the year. There hadn't been a cloud in the sky anywhere he'd looked.

Then the Connells had returned with all the money they'd gotten for their herd in one small buckskin pouch. He remembered old Franklyn Connell's words as plain as day.

"They're giving 'em away at Tucson. A man's lucky to get a dollar a head. I tell you, boys, it's more'n folks can stand. No bolt cloth for the women, no new leather goods for the boys. It's more'n a man can stand, after pulling his guts out for a year to bring his cattle up to the selling point . . . then have to near give 'em away. I'd quit, so help me God, I'd quit in a minute, if I just knew what else to do. I'd hire me out as a plain cowboy . . . only who'd be able to pay me?"

And the wonderfully warm and sparkling spring had run on, its days cloudless, warm, and beautiful, its nights bell-clear and cold. As fine a spring as a man could have asked for, and there lay the deception, because regardless of all those golden days, the cattle market had continued to skid downward. The Pheeters had sent their drive overland, too, with the same results. They had brought back scarcely enough money to see them through the winter to come. But nothing impaired the warmth and the beauty of those dazzling days, nothing at all unless it was the specter of hunger and want and destitution.

Here lay the secret of the thing, but that horseman passing along toward the base of some stiff-standing stone spires, multi-colored and ghostly in the night, had no inkling about that secret. He'd grown from a button on the Perdition Range. He knew how to winter cattle and take the snap out of bronco horses. He could track a man like an Indian and he could make the Journey of the Dead One without worry, but he could not and he did not understand anything at all about the laws governing supply and demand. He had no idea *why* you couldn't give your cattle away, he only knew that you couldn't, and who was there to say this knowledge wasn't, after all, the crux of the whole thing?

There was something else he did know. He'd come near to manhood knowing it. A gun could arbitrate almost any difference. It could even up the biggest odds. It could save a man and the things he believed in. It could rectify such inequalities as his kind now faced. It could fill a man's saddlebags with crisp, cool cash money off the Lordsburg stage with scarcely a word spoken to support its tilted muzzle and its cocked blue-steel hammer.

There was always a way, he told his horse as they skirted on around those multi-colored spires, westbound, all a person had to do was figure it out, then go do it. Maybe in the settlements a man's way wasn't always considered right, but what exactly was right? Right, he confided to the horse, was what a person had to do to protect his own. Right was taking, if there was no other way, in order to be certain no one went hungry next winter. Right was what a man felt in his faithful heart must be done, and that was still another of the benefits of living far from settlements. You did what you had to do. No one interfered, no one scowled. Your own kind understood you were doing right. That's what right was, damn it all.

Beyond the colored spires, around the haunch of an ancient hill, was the broken-to-flowing immensity of Perdition Range. The rider was home, and it wasn't even dawn yet.

CHAPTER TWO

Cap Hanson sat down and said: "Well now, I'll tell you, whoever he was he knew the country. He wasn't a drifter passing through and he wasn't some Lordsburg bum. He knew exactly what he was going to do, how he meant to do it, and where . . . then he did it."

"That," stated Evarts, "is all plain enough without you saying it. Of course he knew what he was going to do. If he hadn't known, he wouldn't have been lying out there waiting for the stage to halt on the upgrade to blow the horses."

Cap Hanson's blue eyes snapped. Jim Evarts was a hard man to like at his best and right now he wasn't trying to be liked. In Hanson's seven years as a captain in the Arizona Rangers he'd met his share of irate businessmen, but few irritated him quite as much as Jim Evarts.

This was not the first meeting of these two men. Evarts, as Lordsburg manager of the Great Western Stage Company's line connecting New Mexico Territory with Arizona Territory, had filed robbery complaints before, and Evarts had never failed to imply that the Arizona Rangers were unfit to catch highwaymen. In fact, although neither man would have admitted it, there was considerable ill will between them.

The third man in that room was Sheriff Darcy Mather, whose county offices were in Lordsburg. Darcy was better than six feet tall, as broad as a barn, moon-faced and gray-eyed. Nothing ever excited or ruffled his stolid composure. He was noted as

14

being absolutely fearless. He was also noted for being an old friend of Cap Hanson's, so now he said to Jim Evarts: "I've told you ten times, Jim, to put an extra guard on those bullion coaches, and to have an outrider go ahead any time the stages are going upgrade like that."

"Talk," snapped Evarts. "Talk. It's no good to say what should've been done, Darcy. It's what's going to be done from here on that I want to know about. There was fifteen thousand dollars in paper currency on that coach. My home office up in Denver is going to blow the roof when they hear about this. I want something definitely encouraging to tell them, and what do I get . . . talk!"

Cap Hanson stood up. He looked at Jim Evarts from hostile eyes. "It only happened last night. You want miracles?"

"No," snarled Evarts, also rising. "I want a robber. More than that, I want our fifteen thousand dollars back."

A sharp roll of knuckles came from beyond the sheriff's office door. Darcy heaved around in his chair and growled for whoever was out there to enter. The door opened and a solidly angular man stepped in, shot a look around, closed the door, and stood with his back to it. This newcomer was a deceptively built man— nature had packed a lot of gristle and stamina under his hide. His gray eyes were dead level from behind the half droop of lids and many a desert sun had deposited its layers of tan smoothly over his face. All his features were solid; all his bodily planes and angles were flat. He was very clearly no ordinary range rider, and yet he dressed as one, stood over there now, looking like one, and when he spoke, his drawling voice had the twang of cow camps and upcountry drives to it.

It was the look in his eyes and the lashed-down way he wore a gun that plainly said this was no ordinary cowboy at all. But, until a person took the time to assess him fully, he seemed like just another saddle man.

He said: "You sent for me, Cap?"

Hanson nodded. "Yeah. Evarts, meet Buck Windsor. Buck's just finished a rustling case down here and I'm going to put him on your stage robbery."

Evarts looked, slightly nodded at Windsor, and looked away, his expression full of distaste, full of something near to scorn.

"You two know each other," Hanson said to Darcy Mather. "No need for an introduction." As Sheriff Mather and Buck Windsor saluted one another with little nods, Cap Hanson addressed himself to Windsor.

"Another of Evarts's Great Western coaches was robbed. Fifteen thousand in paper money was taken off it this time, and the highwayman used his head. Instead of shooting anyone, he waylaid the coach where it came near the crest of the hill north of town. He took the box while the driver was resting his horses, shot the lock off it, stuffed the money into his saddlebags, and rode off."

"Northward?" asked Windsor.

Hanson nodded. "That's what the driver said, but he could've cut out in any direction as soon as he was out of sight. You know how that goes."

Windsor stood expressionless for a moment before saying: "Captain, I'm due for some leave. I've been on the job since last spring without a day off."

Evarts whirled. "Is that all law enforcement means to you?" he challenged.

Windsor's gaze shifted a little. He looked Jim Evarts up and down. "You got a bad habit," he said quietly. "You run off at the mouth, Mister Evarts. Let me give you some advice . . . think what you like, but don't let your tongue get you into trouble."

Evarts glared. He seemed to be balancing some retort to this but in the end he didn't say it. He simply snatched up his hat, spun away, and slammed on out of Darcy Mather's office, his back stiff with outrage, his face gray and unrelenting.

For a little while after Evarts's departure, no one said anything. Darcy Mather heaved up out of his chair, crossed to the stove, and shook the black coffee pot there.

"Anyone for a little java before we break this up?" he asked.

Cap Hanson shrugged. He looked glum and out of sorts. Buck Windsor didn't say anything, either. He was watching Hanson.

"All right," he eventually said, "forget about the time off. Maybe, with anyone but Evarts I'd hold out for it. With him . . . all right, I'll go after his lousy fifteen thousand."

Hanson's features perceptibly brightened. "I'll remember it, Buck. I got a good memory for things like that. Now then, all the driver of that stage said was that this highwayman was about six feet tall, limber-moving like maybe he was a youngish feller, and kept a bandanna over his face. He wore a dark brown hat, a rawhide-braided hatband, had scuffed and run-over old boots, and wore faded Levi's and a faded old blue work shirt. He'd be a cowboy, probably, and he handled his gun like he knew what it was for."

"Did the driver see his horse?"

"Nope. There's a lot of big rocks around that pull out. The horse was hid around there somewhere. You shouldn't have any trouble picking up the trail, though, as long as you get right on it and the weather doesn't change."

"Four points to the compass," Windsor mused. "Which one?"

"North," said Darcy Mather, "or maybe west. Not south because the incoming stage didn't see anyone out that way."

"And east?"

Mather shook his head. "Some Quarter Circle riders came to town from the east, which was a stroke of luck, and they didn't see anyone out there, either."

"North," mused Windsor. "There's nothing up there for three

hundred miles, but dust and desert."

"And death," put in Cap Hanson, "if he doesn't know the country."

"He'd know it, if he went north or west, Cap. He might be desperate but he wouldn't be crazy, and it'd take a crazy man to rush off into the north or west without any idea of what lay in those directions."

Hanson lifted his shoulders and dropped them. He'd lived half a lifetime in the Arizona–New Mexico country. He'd spent nearly all his mature years chasing outlaws. He'd known some he thought were sure enough crazy. Still this was Ranger Windsor's affair now. If Windsor chose to do his manhunting north and west that was his business as long as he got his man. Besides, Windsor knew the country. Maybe that highwayman would get lost and perish, but Buck Windsor wouldn't.

"Sure you won't change your mind," asked Sheriff Mather from over at the stove. "Coffee's ready now."

"He'll change it," said Buck Windsor, gazing at Hanson.

They drank coffee and thought their private thoughts. Darcy brought forth three Mexican cigars from his desk, handed them around, and lit up. "It's been a good spring," he said, puffed a moment, then added: "Except for cattlemen."

Hanson and Windsor watched Mather tilt back his head and let off a thin bluish streamer of smoke. Darcy Mather was nearly as old as Cap Hanson. He'd been around a long time. He knew men.

"A feller might get hurt bad by this drop in cattle prices. I noticed a long time ago that when conditions are good there's less serious crime. When they aren't good . . . like now . . . night riders start showing up."

Buck Windsor finished his coffee, put the cup aside, and squinted at the tip of his cigar. In the same elaborately casual tone and without looking at Mather he said: "Like now, Sheriff, like robbing a Great Western stage, maybe?"

"About like that, yes."

"And, knowing the country as well as the people in it, if you were to just shoot a long guess, where would you say such a night rider might come from?"

Big Darcy Mather was wedged in his chair. His moon face was placid, his steely gray eyes seeming inward, as though he'd been occupied up to now weighing and balancing a lot of relevant alternatives. "North or west like you boys figure. He'd know the country. In fact he'd be a native of it."

Cap Hanson's eyes flicked upward. "Injun? Naw, what . . . ?"

"I didn't say Injun. I said native. White man native, Cap." Mather dropped those imperturbable eyes of his to Hanson, on over to Buck Windsor. "Cowman native, to be specific. Cowman native who's run out of money, got worries up to his ears, and couldn't think of anything else to do but rob a Great Western coach."

Windsor and Hanson exchanged a glance. Windsor said: "Go on. What else?"

"I'm just guessing." Mather made a little self-conscious chuckle. "Just sitting here being thankful I don't have to make that ride, guessing about what you're going to find at the other end of it."

"Go right on guessing," said Windsor. "A man told me one time folks can solve crimes just by kicking a lot of ideas around, piecing things together."

"That so," said Darcy Mather. "Who was he?"

"Doesn't matter now, he's dead."

"That's too bad. You see, I've had that same theory for twenty years."

Cap Hanson emptied his coffee cup and looked impatient. "I've got a stage to catch," he stated abruptly.

Mather and Windsor got the innuendo but neither of them

19

heeded it. "He's a native cowman," said Windsor, "who knows the country. He rode off after the robbery into the northward or westerly desert. Right, Sheriff?"

"Right."

"Fine up to this point. Now, if you were to continue guessing . . . ?"

"Theorizing sounds better."

"Yeah. Now if you were to go on theorizing, where would you hazard a guess his stamping ground is?"

"Well, sir," expounded Darcy Mather, holding the cigar away from his face and looking directly at Buck Windsor, "there's no decent grazing country northward for more miles than he could cross with just one horse, and because he came out of that desert country he'd know that."

"Go on, Sheriff."

"But westerly now, that's a little different. After he crossed those damned final hills and hit the flat country again, he'd swing off westerly and keep on going until he came to the Perdition Range."

Cap Hanson's testy, annoyed look began to dilute, to fade out a little as his facial expression got speculative. But he didn't interrupt. He clamped the cigar between his teeth, leaned back, and seemed suddenly to have forgotten he had a stage to catch.

"The Perdition country has a number of cow outfits in it. Mostly they're family ranches. But there's the Matador, which is the biggest and richest and it's owned by Eastern money men. I wouldn't bother with Matador. I'd start finding out which of those other cowmen were gone from home the day before the robbery and the next night, and maybe even the day following. Y'see, those folks over in the Perdition Range country never go anywhere unless to visit back and forth. It wouldn't be hard to find out who wasn't home."

Buck Windsor put aside his cigar and gazed at Cap Hanson.

"No moon last night," he murmured. "The country westward from the Pinals is open as far as you can see and for ten miles farther than that. It dovetails, Cap. If he came from the Perdition country, he'd surely cross that big open stretch of barren desert on a dark night when no one could possibly see him."

"Or coincidence jumped in and helped," said Cap, taking out a gold watch, opening its cover, and peering at the spidery hands.

"Coincidence didn't knock the bottom out of the cattle market," said Darcy Mather. "Coincidence didn't just happen to turn him back north or west, Cap, directions no one in his right mind would travel even in the springtime. Coincidence didn't. . . ."

"All right, all right Darcy. I'm not arguing with you. I'm just trying to keep you two from getting ahead of yourselves. And I'm not saying the theory of solving crimes by talking doesn't have merits. All I'm suggesting is that Buck better get saddled and ride, because *that's* the only way you apprehend highwaymen. Now I got to catch that stage. Good bye and good luck . . . both of you."

CHAPTER THREE

Buck Windsor entered the Pinals with a reddening late afternoon sun guiding him. He'd picked up tracks where the robbery had taken place, followed them to a lava bed, and lost them there, which was no more than he'd expected to do, but he was satisfied because those tracks led him northward toward the Pinals.

In the foothills he dismounted near a spidery *paloverde* tree to rest his horse briefly, and rummaged his memory for recollections of what lay on across these granite crags. He hadn't had occasion to ride this back country for several years and it wasn't a land that a man would ever willingly recall.

Later, seeking an upward trail, he found one and gauged that far-away sinking sun. He had no wish to be caught up here where one mistake could send a man to his death over glass-like rock pinnacles. He thought he could make it through, and pushed his animal along.

He was doing this for a specific reason. It was Buck Windsor's wish to cross the Pinals and the westerly desert in the dark exactly as he thought his prey might have also done. He did not do this simply to prove that it could be done. He wished to arrive in the Perdition Range country as unannounced as the highwayman had also done—if indeed the highwayman had gone there—which he never could accomplish in broad daylight because a rider moving across that huge empty basin would surely be seen long before he got across it.

When he crested the ramparts, pointed his mount down the north side, he was able to see for many miles all around. Westerly, noticeable now because that sinking sun struck hard against them bringing on a vivid flashing of reflected light, he made out some far-away rocky spires. Beyond them stood a huge plateau, a kind of table-top mountain. Behind that immense butte somewhere lay Perdition Range. He remembered that much.

The sun was dissolving in a saffron mist when he struck the plains again and swung west. He angled back and forth for three-quarters of a mile before he found what he'd hoped might appear—horse tracks leading due west.

After nightfall came, looking across the leagues of this dead, lost world, he could no longer make out those multicolored spires, but it didn't matter. He had a good sense of direction. The important thing now was to get across the desert. Windsor let his animal pick its own gait. The best way to cover ground on horseback was the slow, persevering way. Windsor rode even-balanced in his saddle, as much to favor his horse as for his own comfort.

He passed across a gravelly dry wash where the shod hoofs of his mount made a quiet rattle in the endless silence. He passed by some bleached remnants of a wagon, horse skeletons still harnessed to the tongue. His eyes probed the roundabout gloom, which shone faintly because of mica in the alkali dust to catch and fling back star shine reflection. He speculated upon the probable course of those tracks he'd seen but made no effort to get down and trace them out. There was only one way that unknown horseman could have gone—northward around the butte behind those standing spires.

He passed along unseen, considering what he'd find in Perdition Range country, speculating on the kind of a man who'd robbed Jim Evarts's stage, turning over in his mind the myriad fragments he had to work with. His mind inevitably turned inward as he thought about these things the way lonely men sometimes do.

He was a seasoned manhunter. At twenty-seven he knew most of the tricks pursued men used. He would watch for every one of them. He knew, too, how it was in those insular communities of the back country where outside lawmen were never welcome even though the people did not necessarily hold with outlawry. And he wondered for the hundredth time why he stayed with this manhunting work.

He'd gotten into it by accident. A drifter had stolen his horse. He'd run the man down in a race that had involved no deductive powers at all, only endurance. He'd proven himself tougher than an Apache, more stubborn than most men, and without fear. Afterward, Cap Hanson had brought up the subject of joining the Arizona Rangers. At the time he hadn't been enthusiastic, but he'd needed work, so he'd joined.

Since those days he'd become one of the best men Hanson had. He'd learned the tricks of the manhunter's trade, welded them to his own toughness, and so far no man he'd gone after had gotten away. In fact, Buck Windsor was becoming a legend in the desert country of his native Southwest. Even the other Rangers, all selected for durability, wile, and fearlessness, wagged their heads over his exploits.

He thought of some of the men he'd brought in as he passed across that hushed and empty void. Rustlers, highwaymen, horse thieves, gunmen—and once a woman who'd tried three times to bushwhack him as he stayed on her trail, permitting her no rest and no peace. None of it was pleasant to recall. He got no deep-down feeling of satisfaction other manhunters sometimes got for jobs well done, so, just before he felt the nearness of those onward spires, he switched to other things, other recollections that had helped at one time or another shape and form and sustain his private world.

The night was nearly gone by now, the desert was behind him. He could barely make out that big butte in the ghostly star shine, but he could feel the piled up heat from daytime coming outward to him from it.

When those multicolored spires loomed directly ahead, he halted, got down to rest his horse again, and hunkered, Indian fashion, near his horse's head with one rein loosely held in a scarred fist. Sometimes a man rode thirty miles and got nothing more for his effort than a sore back. Other times a man rode five miles and got everything he wished for. He'd come thirty miles since the evening before. On around the flank of that big plateau another five miles was Perdition Range. Time would tell which it was to be this time, a useless trip in the dark or a hint in the depths of someone's eyes that he was heading in the right direction.

He left the spires behind, rode on around those bony flanks of the butte, and emerged into Perdition Range's great endless sweep of land.

Here, the land was richer. Not much, not enough to grow anything but tough, short grass, and richer than the desert had been. He had some vague idea about that big butte having something to do with this. He knew how the old-time Indians used to climb to the top of buttes like that one and pray for rain, and how very often it afterward rained. He didn't know, but he had a notion that somehow the position of those monolithic places throughout the Southwest had perhaps more to do with rain coming than Apache prayers. It didn't have to be that way, of course, and perhaps the prayers did bring rain, but one thing he knew for a fact—the Indian rain-makers had been taken away long ago, sent to schools, made to put on pants, and it still rained around those big plateaus.

The sky began to grow pale, to push away the lingering murk

of night so that dawn might eventually come. It was a slow process, agonizingly slow up to a point. But when that desert sun finally came, it didn't creep up out of the east as other suns did. It gave a big bound and landed upon the edge of the world, full-grown, dazzling, the size of the biggest wagon wheel imaginable. Its light flashed outward with incomparable swiftness. It burned away the wispy tatters of lingering night out of the secret cañons. It seared a fiery scald over the desert and bounced off the buttes and spires, throwing back a quick, life-giving heat that steadily increased as day wore along until a man and his horse were punished by it.

That's how dawn finally came to Perdition Range. It struck Windsor across the shoulders, kneading his muscles, turning them all loose and flaccid because he was tired. It slowed the onward shuffle of his animal and it danced invitingly over across the grass plain, sharpening the greenness and the drabness, making both appear vastly more enticing than they actually were.

The morning was half gone and the heat had reached its accumulated springtime intensity, which was not actually uncomfortable at all, before Windsor paused. Far ahead but discernible in this winy atmosphere was a set of ranch buildings. He speculated upon them for a while, then decided, before he did any asking around in the Perdition country, to get some sleep. He had the entire day ahead of him; he'd come an uncommon long way; his horse was weary, and so was he. If the outlaw he wanted were hereabout, he'd still be here in the afternoon, or the next day for that matter. And if he weren't here, a tired manhunter on a head-hung horse wasn't going to catch up to him riding along asleep in the saddle.

He went back a little distance to where he'd spotted some tumbled rocks and led his horse there. The way his animal pricked up its ears brought him up to full wariness. There appeared to be something close that absorbed the horse's full interest. That could be anything from another horse to a rutting porcupine—to a man. He left the animal, took his saddle gun, and went clambering and squeezing amid those jumbled great stones until he simultaneously came upon two things. One was an old burial site for an Indian. It had been desecrated by predators; its symbolic painted sticks were broken, knocked down, and trampled. There was a gloomy fissure here; the mummy bundle would be in there.

The second thing was a little clear-water spring as unexpected in this country as the abrupt apparition of a beautiful woman would have been. Clearly the Apaches had known of this spring. Perhaps, since they'd buried one of their own here, they'd attributed magic powers to those waters. One thing was certain. That was just about the clearest, cleanest, most inviting spring Windsor had ever seen. He put aside the carbine, scrambled down to it, kneeled, and tanked up.

It was sweet water, which was another surprise. Normally, in this land of alkali, the water tasted bitter or sulphurous. He filled his hat, took water back to the horse, and took the horse to where his pricked-up ears had led Windsor. He made that trip three times, until the horse was satisfied, then he off-saddled, hobbled the horse, and returned to the spring site for his nap. That was when he saw the faint imprints of boots. He circled around, found two knee-pad imprints, quartered a little more and found where a man had hunkered, had smoked a cigarette, and had laid some saddlebags across an edge of crusty earth.

He hooked one leg over a warm boulder, gazed at those telltale marks, and told himself he hadn't come the full five miles and already he had what he needed to rest peacefully here—the proof that his highwayman had been here, had smoked, had fondled his stolen $15,000 in paper dollars, and had drunk deeply from this spring.

He said aloud, after the habit of men much alone: "That dog-goned Darcy Mather was right. There's one chance out of a thousand . . . out of a million . . . that two men would stumble across this hidden spring the same day, in a land where ten men wouldn't cross over this way in a year. Whoever he is, he's a native all right. Darcy's right sure as night follows day."

He put his hat aside, eased down with his back to an unrelenting granite boulder, closed his eyes, and slept. Not until the sun moved around to burn against his left side did he awaken, and even then he didn't hurry away from this place because, by moving ten feet, he was shielded from the sun by timeless stone, and it was pleasantly still and restful here, while beyond this place from today on, he wouldn't be able for a long time to lie down as thoroughly relaxed as he had here. A manhunter nearing the end of his trail could sense how it was to be, but that required no great powers of divination, for once the law showed up where an outlaw was, the law could hope to survive only by keeping eternally on guard. A man could be simply a stage robber one day, but crowd him and the following day he'd become a killer.

Windsor sighed. For a little while yet he wouldn't have to dredge up all his defenses and his wiles. He pushed the grimmer thoughts out of his mind, and speculated upon that old Apache grave. Who was buried there? What had he done in his lifetime? How many foemen had he stealthily annihilated? A man was like a leaf; the winds of his time blew him first here, then there. They slammed him against bulwarks and they cast him gently into places where a little part of his heart forever after remained. He stood tall sometimes, and he stood small other times.

A lizard jumped out of nowhere, stared grittily at Windsor, jerked its body up and down, puffing itself up, and broke his train of thought with its ludicrous posturing. He took up his hat, arose, dusted his britches, and went on down where his horse stood drowsing. He removed the hobbles, rigged out, stepped up, and swung away from that secret place with its sweet-water spring and its melancholy, ancient grave. But he would remember it.

Twice he cut into and crossed out of worn old cattle trails. There was fresh sign each time of the animals that had used these pathways. A mile along, heading southward out and around those onward ranch buildings, he came upon a wagon's tracks. It looked as though someone had been driving southward. He thought perhaps it was one of the Perdition Range cowmen going to visit a neighbor. As far as he could see, though, there was not another set of buildings anywhere around. Still, in short-grass country like this, ranches were never close; it took a lot of land to support cattle this close to that alkali desert.

Windsor had a plan. He rode west for a long time, until the overhead sun was dropping off center, then he saw another ranch, and slouched along as a man might who'd come all the way from Tucson, farther west. If his particular outlaw was hereabout, and he was almost positive that he was, it would be much better if Windsor seemed to arrive in the Perdition country out of the west instead of out of the east. Bad enough for a stranger to arrive in the country right now, but if someone was watching—and someone surely would be watching—and saw a stranger coming along from the direction of Lordsburg, that stranger would be in a peck of trouble before he even got a chance to make up a good story.

The ways of the hunted and the hunter, Windsor thought as he rode along, rarely changed. It was almost as though the entire business of fleeing and pursuing followed some rigid and ancient pattern. It was a little like playing checkers—first the outlaw made his illegal move, then the law made *its* move. Then the outlaw moved again and the law tried to anticipate or counteract that move.

Finally, when someone's back was to the wall, one man or the other, then the rules changed and the game was no longer strictly a game at all, it became a matter of killing or being killed. Sometimes one of them would surrender, worn down and demoralized, but not often, providing the outlaw was hardened to his profession, as hardened as the manhunter was. Then someone died.

CHAPTER FOUR

There were a dozen ways to attract attention in a strange country but just about the best way was to start a fire. Even in the springtime when no one feared fire, spiraling smoke brought out the curious or the suspicious, because in the springtime in cow country calves were dropped, and enterprising loose-rope artists often began acquiring the nucleus of their herds then—by branding other folks' calves before the owners could get around to it.

Buck gathered twigs near an outthrust of a lava fault that came abruptly out of the flinty soil, built his little fire there, tossed enough green grass on the flames to insure rising smoke, then rummaged his saddlebags for food, which he proceeded to prepare. Ordinarily he'd have eaten this meal cold. Actually, when he had to make meals himself, he was indifferent about how they were prepared. He was not a good cook, never had been, could not seem to learn to be, and he knew this better than anyone else knew it, so he always carried in his saddlebags whatever could be eaten cold and hastily.

But now he cooked a warm meal. Afterward, he tossed on more grass, put his back to the lava rock outthrust, tilted his hat, and dozed. The day was aging; morning's dazzling blush had become midday's somber haziness, and when Buck opened his eyes, peering from beneath his hat brim without moving or seeming even to breathe, that rusty, reddening afternoon hue was beginning to color the Perdition country from west to east, from north to south.

He'd heard the horse coming. He'd listened to it with the skepticism he'd used often in his lifetime when in strange places, a mixture of interest and caution. He did not move. His back was to the warm lava rock, his legs were thrust out their full length, and his shoulders drooped. He was a picture of a sleeping man, of a rider worn down with much weariness.

Horse and rider came on around from the west. They passed around Windsor from behind. They did not approach at once. Instead, they made a wide circle northerly, ending up off in the nearby west, opposite Windsor. There, they halted. He could see them; it was no accident his hat brim did not impair his vision.

He watched the rider get down carefully. He was an Indian, an Apache cowboy, and his head and chest were much too massive for his little, spindly, incongruous legs.

He was a young man, a year or two younger than Windsor. His cheeks were pockmarked, muddy-colored to match the whites of his eyes, and he now showed startlingly white teeth in a thin, speculative grin.

Buck knew what that cowboy was going to do. It was a very old game among Apaches; at other times it had not been funny at all. Many a settler, a Mexican faggot gatherer or sheepherder, had died in frantic agony when Apaches had played their particularly derisive trick on them in the old days.

They would catch a man asleep or off guard. They would stalk him. Sometimes it would take them two hours, sometimes ten hours, but they would lie motionlessly, then glide forward an inch at a time until they got up to within six or eight inches of the man. If he'd been a sheepherder in the old days, they'd often bring one of the little bells off one of his ewes. They would rise up absolutely without a sound, squat there six inches from the sleeping man, grinning, and tinkle that little bell in his face; tinkle it until the man, thinking one of his ewes was in camp,

would open his eyes to see her, perhaps to toss a stick at her—
and there would be grinning death in its most frightening form
holding up the little bell in one hand, his butchering knife in
the other hand.

It was an old game. Buck watched the Apache squat, still
grinning, remove his spurs, put aside his black hat, and start
stalking. Buck made it easy for the Indian cowboy. Even when
there was a faint rustling in the grass, he slept on unheedingly.

The Apache grew careless. It was obvious that his victim was
a deep sleeper. He paused near the fire, cast a long, wondering
look downward at Windsor's saddlebags, and just when Buck
was certain the man was going to plunder them, the cowboy
came on again. He made more noise now, his certainty of
Windsor's fathomless sleep absolutely unshaken. He was less
than a foot away when Windsor spoke to him.

"Look down, friend, at my right hand." The Indian froze,
taken entirely by surprise. "It's a good thing we were just playing a game. Otherwise, you'd be flapping your way up to heaven
by now to see your ancestors."

Windsor reached up with his left hand, flicked back his hat,
and smiled a little. In his right hand, as though it had appeared
there of its own volition, was Windsor's cocked six-gun.

Windsor put up the gun, shoved forward off the lava rock,
and said: "Care for some coffee?"

The Apache cowboy recovered, dropped a string of swear
words, and rose up to regard Windsor from humiliated eyes.
Windsor stepped around to where he was facing the cowboy
across his little fire, hunkered down, and poured his tin cup full.
"Here," he said, offering it upward. "Forget about the other
thing. I'll never talk about it."

The Apache took the cup, dropped down on his heels, and
ruefully shook his head. "You're pretty good," he finally said.
"I'd've been a dead buck Injun for sure if that had been for

keeps." The man drank, wiped his lips, and flickered his black eyes over Windsor, over his horse nearby, his outfit there by the fire, and back to Windsor's face again. "You passing through from Tucson?"

"Yeah."

"Looking for work?"

"Maybe," said Windsor. "What's the outfit?"

"Matador Land and Cattle."

"I've heard of 'em. Big outfit."

"Biggest along the Mex border."

"Owns the whole country I've heard."

The Apache cowboy put down Windsor's cup and shook his head. "No. There are some private outfits around here, too. Not very big, any of 'em, but altogether they may run two, three thousand head." The Indian showed his amazingly perfect teeth again; in contrast to his dusky hide they seemed white as snow. "They're having a hard time of it, though. Some of 'em took cattle to Tucson and couldn't give 'em away."

"Yeah, I know. The whole place is full of cowmen groaning and moaning."

The cowboy continued to grin, but his snake-like, jet-black eyes behind layers of puckered flesh were like daggers. They probed and assessed and totaled up what they saw across that dying little fire.

"The boss might put you on," he eventually said. "If you're as good with a rope as you are with that gun, I figure he will. Anyway, I need a riding pardner out here."

The Indian lifted one short, powerful arm and gestured with it. While he was looking away, Buck did a little appraising of his own. The Apache wasn't more than five feet six inches tall but he weighed within a pound or two of what Buck also weighed. He was compact, massive, deep-chested, and villainous-looking, except when he smiled, then he appeared raffishly good-natured.

He was, Buck thought, no more than one generation removed from the blanket and the brush shelter. He would be a rough, sly, confident man who cared nothing for many facets of civilized life. Yet he was typical enough of his breed to be intensely loyal and utterly fearless. There were some Apache attributes mission schools and the white man's environment would never completely winnow out of the Apache spirit. Those last two factors were among them.

"It's a big country," said the Apache cowboy. "Matador beef critters are all over it. My boss is Tom Douglas. He's range boss for the north country . . . for the Perdition Range country. Our main camp and wagons are about six miles south of here." The Indian dropped his arm, swung back to face Windsor, and said: "My name is Tick."

Windsor raised his eyebrows. "Tick?"

"Yeah. In Mex, *garrapata*. Woodtick. For short they call me Tick." The Apache smiled again and faintly shrugged. "It's easier to say Tick than to say Clarence or something like that, isn't it?"

Windsor matched that smile with a little grin of his own. "Sure, and if you don't mind, I sure don't. My name's Buck Windsor."

The Apache stood up. "One thing, Buck," he said, those jet eyes of his running over Windsor in that skeptical, considering way again. "If you're passing through for your health, don't let Tom Douglas find out about it. He doesn't like dodgers."

Buck started pushing things back into his saddlebags. He said nothing until he'd finished. He stood up, put the saddlebags carelessly over one shoulder, and looked straight across at Tick.

"Glad you told me," he murmured, paused a moment, then said: "Let's go meet your boss." He had deliberately left the question open whether he was running from the law or not. In his experience as a manhunter he'd long ago come to the conclusion that if men were always a little doubtful, they made a point to step lightly, and that was the way he wanted it.

They got astride and rode southward. Once, where they passed far out from the visible buildings, Tick said, with a casual wave: "The Pheeters place. One of those Perdition Range cowmen I told you about. He took a drive to Tucson and came back without the cattle and little else."

Buck peered over at those buildings. They seemed old, badly weather-checked, and run-down. "Pheeters been in the country long?" he asked, knowing what the answer would be from the look of those buildings before Tick replied.

"Since the old days. He doesn't like Injuns." Tick made a crooked grin with his lips, but his eyes showed no warmth or amusement. "Had a brother once . . . he got killed."

Tick didn't enlarge on this. Buck guessed why. Tick was a tame Apache, but he knew things, remembered boasts he'd heard as a child. He knew more about the killing of Pheeters's brother than he'd tell. There were a lot of these second-generation tame Apaches like that. Among men like Pheeters they were disliked and distrusted.

Buck said mildly: "Sometimes it takes many years." He didn't say *what* took many years.

Tick looked over at him. "Yeah," he said dryly.

"Pheeters go with his drive over to Tucson?"

"He went. I sat out a ways and watched them. Old Buster and his boy. The other boy didn't go."

Buck's interest quickened. "How many kids has old Buster got?"

"Just the two boys. The one that didn't go is sweet on Franklyn Connell's girl, Jennie. S'pose he hung back so's he could have a free rein riding over to the Connell place."

"Where's that?"

Tick waved an arm backward by way of answer and Buck,

recalling that first set of buildings he'd seen, nodded. He was beginning to get the lay of this country. Then Tick spoke again.

"Micah's spending a lot of time over at the Connell place. I've seen him coming and going every week for the past month. Franklyn'll run him off one of these days."

"Micah? Pheeters's other son?"

"The youngest one. The one with hair the color of straw. He's sweet on Jennie, like I told you." Tick turned, made a slow, sly smile, and said: "Night before last I was bedded down about a half mile north of where I met you today. I heard a horse and woke up. . . ." Tick's perfect white teeth flashed knowingly but he said no more, just kept grinning over at Buck.

"Micah?" asked Buck.

"Yeah. Hell, it was near dawn. If old Franklyn Connell knew that, he'd skin Micah alive and maybe take a willow to his girl in the bargain."

Tick had a little more to say but Buck wasn't paying attention. He was fitting young Micah Pheeters into the rôle of a stage robber. The time was about right, providing young Pheeters didn't tarry on the return trip from over near Lordsburg. The direction was right, too. If Tick was wrong in his guess about where young Micah had been, Buck had his work cut out for him. That might take a little finding out but he was up to it.

Shadows dropped around them. Far ahead a cooking fire showed richly orange. Tick said: "That's camp. I'll take you to meet Tom."

CHAPTER FIVE

Tom Douglas was one of those men nature had fashioned for only one environment, and he was in it now. He was a raw-boned, large man with dark eyes, a taciturn, almost surly manner, and two prominent knife scars on his face. He rarely smiled and never laughed. He looked hard-fisted and iron-willed, and he was both. He'd fought the last of the old hold-out Apaches in his youth. He'd battled Mexican marauders up over the line many times, and he'd picked up those facial scars in a Tularosa saloon in a brawl involving two Texans with knives.

Tom was known and respected all along the border. When Tick took Buck Windsor over to introduce him, Tom was standing with his back to the fire, holding a cup of coffee. He looked closer to seven feet tall than the actual six two that he was, and firelight made the high cheek bones in his face look bronzed, appearing more Indian than anything else.

"You said I needed a pardner in the north," stated Tick. "Well, here he is." Tick turned and started away. Tom Douglas halted him with three words.

"Come back here."

Tick returned. Those two exchanged a long look at one another. Tick showed no fear, no trepidation of any kind, and Buck admired him for this because Tom Douglas outweighed Tick by fifty pounds and towered nearly a foot above him.

Douglas had big-roweled Mexican spurs on his heels and a silver-overlaid Mexican six-gun in his battered old hip holster, obviously the plunder from some border scuffle.

"I'll tell you who rides the north range with you. You don't bring in some feller and tell me."

Thus far Douglas hadn't more than flicked a glance over Buck, and around the three of them other Matador men paused at their supper to look and listen, their faces alternately brightened by the fire, and plunged into nighttime sootiness.

"Forget it," said Buck roughly to Tom Douglas. He turned as though to go. He was indignant at Douglas for humiliating Tick before all those other men.

But Douglas turned a little and said: "Hold it, mister. I'm not through yet."

Buck turned. There were fire points in his eyes that none of those Matador men could see in the night. "As far as I'm concerned you're through," he stated icily. "I wouldn't work for an outfit that puts a man like you over other men."

"No?" said Tom Douglas, keeping Buck stockstill with his cold, crisp, dark stare. "You think I ought to hire you just because Tick brings you here?"

"I didn't ask you to hire me, mister. And if you don't have any more respect for the fellows who ride for you than you've shown here tonight . . . why then, I wouldn't ride for your lousy Matador outfit if it was the last outfit in the world."

"You're pretty free with your thoughts, mister," said Tom Douglas, his expression turning iron-like toward Windsor.

"And I can back 'em up, too," ground out Buck, cold with anger. "Maybe you'd like to try me."

Now those Matador cowboys by the fire began moving up. Some, seated cross-legged in front of the chuck wagon, soberly put aside their tin plates, their coffee cups, and began heading around the fire toward Windsor. One of them, an old hand with a grizzled, gray look to him, said softly: "Easy, young feller, easy. You're not in the best place in the world to make war talk.

You touch that gun and you'll get yourself cut to pieces."

Buck didn't touch the gun. He had no intention of touching it, because in Tom Douglas's scarred face he'd seen no acceptance of his challenge. In fact, Douglas, except for looking expressionlessly at Buck, had not so much as blinked an eye.

Now he said to that gray and grizzled older man: "It's all right, Cuff. Slack off, fellers. Our visitor with the short fuse isn't going to do anything foolish." Douglas twisted, handed his emptied coffee cup to a cowboy, and twisted back.

"Thirty a month and found," he said to Buck. "You ride the Perdition Range country up north with Tick. Matador pays once a month . . . last day of each month." Douglas paused. He watched Buck's firelit face a moment, then said: "Mister, if you're on the dodge, I don't want you. Are you?"

"No I'm not."

"Good. Then get settled in, spend the night here, and in the morning head back up north with Tick. And, mister. . . ."

"Yeah?"

Tom Douglas softly shook his head at Buck. "It's a good thing you didn't try it," he said, and turned on his heel, passed around the fire, and faded out in the gloom over by the chuck wagon.

Buck with a hard retort to Douglas's last statement on the tip of his tongue never got a chance to say it. That gray and grizzled cowboy walked up, blew out a big breath, and gave his head a melancholy wag. "Calm down," he said to Buck. "Tom's the best man in these parts, mister. When he said it's a good thing you didn't try it, he was tellin' you the gospel truth."

Buck stifled most of his anger but not all of it. "Yeah," he growled at the older man, "with ten riders to back him up maybe, but not man to man."

The grizzled rider lifted his eyebrows, ran a slow look up and down Buck, pursed his lips, and shrugged. "Maybe," he admitted, "and maybe not. I'll tell you one thing, though. We're none of us ever goin' to find out whether you could take Tom or not, because you plain ain't goin' to try. Now give me your name for the pay book, and after that you 'n' Tick get some grub at the wagon."

Buck complied. He and Tick got plates of beans and sow belly over at the chuck wagon, took them to a place slightly apart from the other Matador men, and squatted down to eat. The other cowboys were finishing up. One brought forth a mouth organ, blew it, and called for another rider, a downy-faced lad named Chet, to fetch his banjo. These two played range songs for a while, then switched over and began playing old marching songs from the war.

Tick leaned over once and said: "Buck, I was holding my breath. They'd have killed us sure if you'd gone for your gun. Maybe you're fast, but no one's fast enough to outshoot ten guns."

Buck looked around. It hadn't been the Apache's fight. If anyone had started it, big Tom Douglas had. "You'd have bought in?" he asked.

"I brought you here, didn't I?" exclaimed Tick, and said no more, but sat back listening to the music.

That grizzled older range rider came over eventually, dropped down, and offered Buck his tobacco sack. Buck declined the offer, watched the older man twist up a smoke with elaborate concentration, and waited. The grizzled rider had something on his mind. He lit up, exhaled, looked idly over at the musicians, and said: "My name's Kennedy. Cuff Kennedy. I boss the south range down along the line. Tom Douglas is over-all range boss for Matador in this area. Most of my area's in New Mexico. Tom's is nearly all in Arizona." Having delivered himself of this orientation course, Cuff Kennedy turned slowly and stared at

Buck. "I've seen you somewhere before." He let that lie between them.

Buck simply said: "Maybe. I've been in these parts a long time."

Kennedy's pale gaze didn't waver. It was obvious he was struggling mightily to recall where he'd seen Windsor before. Tick, lying back with his head propped up on one hand, watched these two, his black spidery gaze missing nothing.

"It'll come to me," said Kennedy after a while. He changed expression and looked on over at the Apache. "How're things goin' up north?" he asked.

"Like always," replied Tick. "Quiet."

"That's the way we like things, isn't it, Tick?"

The Indian didn't answer. He simply yawned and lay fully back, placing both arms under his head, staring straight up at the high heavens.

Kennedy made a dry little smile and returned his attention to Buck. "He's real talkative sometimes. I paired off with him once a few years back. Before I got sent to the south line I was talkin' to myself, and answerin', too. Tick's a good hand, but if he doesn't drive you crazy, you're made of iron."

Buck said nothing to this. Tick rolled his head over, stared blankly at Cuff Kennedy, rolled it back, and continued to gaze at the high sky.

Tom Douglas strode in out of the southward night, said something curt to the musicians, who at once put up their instruments, and continued on over where Buck and Tick were sitting with Cuff Kennedy. He stood a while just looking, then he dropped down and held out a hand. Cuff tossed the tobacco sack into it. Douglas bowed his neck until his face was hidden behind the graceful curl of a hat brim, went to work manufacturing a cigarette, and said to Buck: "Tick will show you cattle from time to time that got no business on Matador range. You'll

42

push em' off." Douglas lit up, exhaled, and raised his head. That dark gaze of his had a shocking directness; it sent a thrill through Buck now, with its coldness, its impersonal efficiency. "Maybe the settlers up there'll snarl a little at you. Sometimes they do when they catch Matador men keeping their animals off our range. Don't pay any attention to that, just keep the damned cattle off."

Buck nodded. He didn't like this man. He could appreciate his hardness and even the necessity for it, but that didn't abrogate his dislike, so instead of answering Douglas he simply nodded.

Off to one side Tick watched these two. He seemed to sense the antagonism here. He also seemed to enjoy it because his glittering black eyes with their muddy whites gleamed approvingly in the night.

"There's the Pheeters bunch up in the Perdition country," went on Douglas, "and old Franklyn Connell. There are others but only Connell and Pheeters make it a point to sneak critters onto Matador grass."

Now Tick spoke up. "Not this spring. Not so far, anyway. There's plenty of feed. It was last year when things were dry that they pushed their cattle onto Matador grass."

Douglas, studying the tip of his cigarette, seemed not to have heard Tick. "You watch sharp," he ordered Buck. "Any time you see critters other than Matador on our land up there, run 'em to hell off. Aside from that Tick'll show you what else is to be done up there. He's got a camp established, got it stocked good, too, from the way he keeps coming down here begging supplies."

Tick smiled in the darkness. Only his startlingly white teeth were visible. Tom Douglas killed his smoke, put a sideward glance toward Buck, and stood up. "I'll tell you why I hired you, mister. You got a temper. I need a man like that on the

Perdition Range. That Pheeters outfit is salty." Douglas turned and walked back toward the chuck wagon. For a little while after he'd departed no one spoke. Then Cuff Kennedy also stood up. He dusted his britches with more concentration than was customary and said quietly while he was doing this: "Windsor, he's a good man. Hold your tongue long enough to find out. He'll back you to the limit any time, any place, once he cottons to you. Well, s'long. I'll be gone back to my own camp before sunup. Maybe we'll meet again."

"Yeah," said Buck. "Good night." He watched Kennedy move off, saw how saddle-warped the older man's legs were, and grunted aloud. "Quite an outfit you work for," he murmured to Tick without looking around at the Apache. "Everyone makes a point of being as tough as they can."

"Got to. Matador's got a lot of country, the best range. Outsiders keep pushing cattle onto us. Got to be tough." Tick yawned, stretched mightily, and afterward tipped up his hat. "You'll find out," he said, composing himself for sleep. "You'll find out the first time you run across old Connell or Buster Pheeters." Tick yawned again. "Why you think I brought you down here for Tom to hire? Because you showed me this evening that you're greased lightning with a gun, and that's exactly the kind of riding pardner I need up there."

"Countryside looked peaceable enough to me," said Buck.

"It is peaceable. It's peaceable as long as Matador riders travel in pairs and get by on Matador's reputation for toughness."

Buck looked down and around. Tick's face was hidden beneath his hat. "Hell of an Injun you are," Buck mumbled.

Tick said wearily: "Yup. Hell of an Injun. How about going to sleep now? We've got to be out of here come sunup, or Tom'll light fires under us."

"Tom," growled Buck, easing back upon the ground, "can go suck eggs."

For a while Tick was silent, then he said drowsily: "Cuff was right, what he told you. Tom's a good man."

"He damned near bit your head off tonight. You forgotten that already?"

"Sure I've forgotten it. I knew he'd do that before we rode in."

Buck, thinking back now, understood why Tick had stood there unflinchingly while Douglas had choused him up one side and down the other. These men understood one another. They were tough and unbending. When Buck had been angered because he'd thought Douglas had deliberately humiliated Tick before the other Matador men, he'd been mistaken. That had simply been part of the ritual of being members of the Matador crew.

He began to see Tom Douglas in a different light. If this did not make him like Douglas any better, at least it helped him understand the man.

He heaved up onto one side, said—"Good night."—to Tick, got back no reply, and closed his eyes. His last conscious thought was one of secret gratification. He'd gotten safely into the Perdition Range country, and that was half the battle.

CHAPTER SIX

One thing Tom Douglas had said there at the southward Matador camp proved no exaggeration at all. When Tick led Buck into his cow camp the following day about noon, Buck laughed out loud.

This camp was made amid huge boulders not far from that secret spring and the overhead huge plateau Buck had encountered the day before. Tick had secreted canned goods in the rocks like a pack rat. He even had several treasured plugs of Day's Work chewing tobacco, although he did not chew tobacco at all.

When Buck laughed, the Indian turned with a smile and said: "Well, you never know about tomorrow, and once you've been bad hungry in your life, you never forget how it is to be without food."

Buck got down, turned his animal loose, and afterward went in among the tumbled huge rocks. Tick watched him from a little cooking fire where he was rustling them a noon day meal.

"Used to be Injun place," he called up to Buck. "They used to sit up there on the top-most rocks and watch both ways . . . behind us out on the Perdition Range, and easterly the way you're looking, over toward Lordsburg. If anything moved, they flashed signals with bits of glass to war parties. After that. . . ." Tick raised and lowered his shoulders.

Buck stair-stepped his way to a flat spire and halted there, looking northwest. After a while he called downward: "Don't have a piece of glass to signal you with, oh mighty chieftain, but damned if someone isn't moving a little bunch of cattle on the Matador range, going south with 'em." Buck looked down where Tick was standing erect, half twisted around, his dark face concerned. "What d'you say, little Geronimo, shall we go make a big raid?"

Tick said: "Come down offen there. Let's go." He did not mimic the old-time ways as Buck was doing at all, and later, as Buck came out of the rocks to get astride, Tick said: "Tom told you what to expect. This'll likely be the Pheeters crew, old Buster and his two boys. Like Tom said, they're salty."

Buck reined around. "And also as Tom said, run 'em off Matador range."

The pair of them loped westward with Buck leading. He surmised that, at the rate he'd seen those cattle and their drovers moving down from the north, he and Tick would intercept them almost due west from the cow camp, and he was quite correct.

But their arrival in the area was observed and three men, two lanky and young, one shorter, broader, and older, came together behind the cattle and seemed to speak hastily back and forth. Buck ignored the cattle, which were mottled, sharp-horned Durham crosses, and concentrated on the men. One of those riders in particular was a man he wished to study. The young one who Tick had told him he'd seen riding hard for home in the small hours of the night after the Lordsburg robbery.

They were approaching those wooden-faced, motionless horsemen when Tick edged in close, leaned out of the saddle, and quietly said: "Watch that lanky, older boy. He's hot-tempered. So is old Buster."

Buck gazed at those two, read violence and defiance in their bronzed, tough-set faces, and switched his attention back to Micah, he of the unruly straw-colored hair, the willful blue stare, and the boyish mouth and cheeks. When he and Tick got up close, Buck gravely nodded and said—" 'Afternoon, gents."—in a civil tone.

None of the Pheeters answered this, but the wiry, wispy, oldest man inclined his head a little, then crossed both hands atop his saddle horn and waited for Buck to say more. Buck did.

"Probably a mistake," he said easily, conversationally, "but you're on Matador range. My pardner and I got orders last night to turn back outside cattle."

"That so," said old Buster Pheeters, studying Buck with curiosity. "You ain't much particular about who you ride with, mister. That feller you call your pardner's a cussed 'Pache. Few years back us white men killed 'em on sight like we killed any other varmint."

Buck's easiness seemed to atrophy. He fixed that tough, small man with an even regard and said: "We're discussing trespassing cattle, Mister Pheeters, not how things were thirty years back."

Now the older of Buster Pheeters's sons spoke up. He was a hard, arrogant, raw-boned man in his early thirties. "You're a newcomer hereabout," he said to Buck. "And if I was you, I'd step right easy until you get the lay of things, cowboy."

"You're not me," said Buck shortly, taking an instant dislike to this one. "Turn your critters and head 'em back off Matador grass."

This was an order and a brusquely given one at that. Those three rough-looking men stared over at Buck, each according to his own values, measuring Windsor. Suddenly the older son swung his right leg over and slid to the ground. Without a word he removed his hat, settled it upon his saddle horn, unbuckled his gun belt, and let it fall. When he was through doing these things, he looked up and said: "There's sure enough a difference between us, mister. Get off that damned horse and let's see just how big a difference there really is."

Buck had a decision to make. He looked over at old Buster, read bleak approval in the old man's seamed and weathered face, looked on past where young Micah sat up there like a statue, looking uncertain and troubled, then nodded his head, having come to his hard conclusion.

"Sure," he said, and stepped down, shucked his shell belt and hat, looked once over to where Tick was impassively watching the old man and young Micah. "I don't know what rules you fellows got about things like this on Perdition Range, but where I grew up we kept it man to man."

Old Buster said shortly: "It's the same here, mister. No one'll interfere." Old Buster looked at his elder son. "Chew him up, Lige," he murmured. "Chew him up and spit him out."

Lige smiled. It was a thoroughly confident, thoroughly savage smile. He brought up two big, scarred fists and minced forward in a circling, measuring way. Within ten seconds he'd revealed himself as a seasoned brawler. He made no rushes, no wasted motions of any kind; he simply moved in and out, always circling, and Buck understood his strategy. He meant to get his adversary maneuvered so that afternoon's sizzling sunlight was in his eyes.

But Windsor was not exactly a novice at this, either. Although he was nearly a head shorter than Lige Pheeters, he wasn't giving anything away in weight and his shorter arms were massively muscled to match the rippling shoulders that backed them up. Tick, as well as old Buster and young Micah, waited, unable to arrive at any obvious conclusions yet. It would be a fierce fight, that much was obvious, but which battler had the edge none of them would have dared say thus far.

Buck, understanding the strategy behind Lige Pheeters's movements, kept stepping sideways. This forced Lige to change course, to move back, and he didn't like doing this. It didn't dawn on Lige what Buck was doing for a while. When it did, when he realized he could not force Buck around into the dazzling sun, Lige paused, reconsidered from behind his raised fists, then started directly in at his adversary.

Buck surmised Pheeters's thinking again. Lige, larger, with a longer reach, was going to turn solidly aggressive. Buck altered his own method accordingly. When Lige got in, swung, and danced back, Buck went under that blow. He afterward dropped both hands, smiled over at Pheeters, and dolorously wagged his head. He said nothing, but it was apparent to Tick, to old Buster and young Micah, that Buck was being derisive. What was not apparent to them was that Buck was deliberately baiting Lige, deliberately seeking to draw the taller man into some exasperated and angry movement.

Lige cocked his right fist again, dropped his right shoulder down behind it, and started in once more. This time, though, he lowered his left. Buck saw and understood; that poised right was to feint with. The left would be what Buck must watch, and he did. He let Lige get close, then launched himself forward in a savage attempt to beat the larger man to the punch.

Lige's cocked right lashed out. His left, with Lige's full weight twisting in behind it upon the balls of the taller man's feet, sizzled in low and powerful.

Buck got past the left and under the right. He had moved in a flash of blurred speed. He struck Lige over the heart. He sank a fist wrist-deep into Lige's middle, breaking the other man's breath out in a loud explosion. He struck upward with a sledging strike that cracked against Lige's long jaw like a pistol shot, then he jumped back out again and half turned to force Lige around, force the injured man in his near stupor to face into that bitter yellow sun. Lige came around without full control of his senses. He moved stolidly and blinked his watering eyes. He was hurt but instinct kept him upright and willing. When the

sunlight struck, blinding him, Lige seemed drowsily to understand his mistake. But it was too late.

Buck came again with both battering fists working in and
out, up and down. He beat Lige until the large man's arms fell,
until his eyes rolled up aimlessly, and his battered mouth gaped
open. Still, Pheeters would not go down. Buck caught Lige by
the shirt front, cocked a fist, stopped in mid-motion, staring
into those unfocussed eyes, gradually, almost reluctantly lowered
that cocked fist, and let go. Lige stood there weaving; he didn't
fall. In fact, he never did go down.

Buck stepped away, drew in a rattling big breath, expelled it,
and looked out where Lige's father sat like stone, his pale eyes
milky and his bloodless, thin lips showing a rind of white around
them.

"You got a canteen on your saddle," Buck told that old man.
"Pour some of it over him, then turn those damned cattle and
get 'em off Matador grass!"

Tick handed Buck his hat, his gun belt, and the reins to his
horse. Tick was watching old Buster and young Micah with his
right hand lying lightly upon a holstered six-gun. Tick was satisfied. He meant to make deadly certain the Pheeterses were also
satisfied.

Buck finished buckling on the shell belt, adjusting his holstered six-gun. He ran bent fingers through his hair and crushed
the hat atop his head. Across from him youthful Micah Pheeters
had dismounted at a growl from his father to walk forward and
pour water over his brother. Buck had this excellent close-up
opportunity to study the younger man. It shocked him to notice
that Micah wasn't over eighteen or nineteen years of age. Much
too young to be a seasoned highwayman. He flexed bruised,
skinned knuckles and looked morosely at them. Darcy Mather
was right again. The stage robber was a native, a cowman, and
in bad straits. One look at the clothing, at the cracked, worn-

out old boots of Micah, of Lige, and of old Buster showed how it was with the Pheeters outfit.

Buster looked over the heads of his tall sons and said: "Mister, what's your name? I want to remember you real good."

Buck turned without at once replying, stepped up over leather, carefully adjusted his reins, and said his name. Then he said: "Pheeters, let it end right here. I'm willing to. Your boy asked for what he got. I didn't push him into it. Take my advice and let it end here."

Old Buster's bronzed, wrinkled face turned hard and hating. His slitted, pale gaze pushed up against Buck. "You was lucky, cowboy, that's all, and you know it. That's why you're willin' to call it quits. Well, with us Pheeterses don't no man ride roughshod over us and that's the end of it. You bought yourself some right worthwhile enemies, Windsor. We got long memories. We also got plenty of guns."

Buck, listening, seeing the stubbornness in that craggy old face, said no more until Micah had helped Lige back into the saddle, which was no simple undertaking. If Micah hadn't possessed unusual strength, he never would have been able to accomplish it. But he did, and Lige, coming out of his stupor a little, instinctively balanced himself up there as Micah turned to cross around to his own animal. Buck was looking straight at Micah when he said: "All right, Buster, have it your way. Any time you want to renew things, just trespass on Matador grass again. But if you don't come, I won't trespass onto Perdition Range."

Buck waited until those three turned, old Buster and young Micah making a long sweep southward to pick up their cattle, and started back the way they had come. He kept his assessing gaze upon the youngest of those rough men until Tick broke in upon his thoughts.

"Maybe you just could whip Tom Douglas. Just maybe you

could, at that. You done a lot of fighting with your hands."

Buck turned, cast a wry look at the Indian, and said: "I'm hungrier'n a denned-up bear. What was that you were cooking back there at the camp . . . fried lizards?"

Tick wagged his head and turned to ride along beside Buck. He grinned a little, saying: "Naw, no fried lizards, white man. That was settler livers with Mex beans."

They laughed together and walked their horses back down the land, Tick privately recapitulating that fight and coming to some shrewd and thoughtful conclusions, while Buck, with the battle behind him, was dwelling almost sadly upon the appearance of young Micah Pheeters, the man he thought was a fair bet to be the highwayman he was in the Perdition Range country to apprehend. He thought he'd slip out this night after Tick was asleep and do a little scouting of the countryside. There was one disadvantage to having a partner, even a rugged and loyal one like Tick. It seriously impaired what he was here to ascertain.

CHAPTER SEVEN

The moon was a sliver with two inward-curving needle-like points that night, in a setting of diamond-bright flickering stars. Tick was bedded down, and for the second night Buck had bedded down beside the Apache. Tick had not undressed, had not even kicked off his boots that most range men shed when they slept even though they might not shed much else.

He waited until Tick's breathing was rhythmically even, then got up, slipped out where their animals were, before putting on his boots, his hat, and gun, and rigging out his horse. It wasn't very late then, no more than perhaps 9:30 or 10:00, but the world was wrapped in darkness and a great depth of silence.

He rode northward, away from their camp, stopped once far out to listen, then resumed his way, satisfied Tick had not discovered his absence, satisfied the Apache was not following him.

He got over onto the Pheeters' range and made a leisurely survey of it. The buildings were, even in that charitable light, exactly as he'd surmised from an earlier sighting. They were run-down-looking, old, and badly weather-checked. But old Buster had built them to last, and to survive Indian attacks. They were closely grouped, planned so that defenders could, with reasonable safety, get from one to the others. The log barn had loopholes along the front loft wall. Even the house, obviously the dwelling place of men only, showed in its frugal plainness and functional ugliness that nothing short of a cannon

54

could rout defenders.

In the moonlight the place looked even grimmer up close than it had appeared from a distance in broad daylight. It reminded Buck of old Buster with its cragginess and its trenchant durability. But he wasn't thinking of Buster. He wasn't even considering battered and surly Lige Pheeters. He was wondering about young Micah.

He couldn't quite rid himself of that hauntingly youthful and troubled face with its vital blue gaze and straw-colored hair even as he was riding on around the Pheeters Ranch, bound for the ranch of Franklyn Connell. He did not believe old Buster would approve of stage robbery even in his present straits. Old Buster was of that oaken breed of frontiersmen who hated with a stubborn passion, who did not compromise with what they considered to be wrong and evil, and who kept their powder dry. He would fight like a lion for his own; he would be unforgiving, but he would scorn dishonesty. Although his cattle had suddenly become worthless and destitution stared him in the face, old Buster would stare right back and cling to his principles. He would not compromise. Buck had read that much in old Buster's face after the fight.

Lige, he thought, as he passed silently along northward, might be different from old Buster. Lige was a man with no set principles; he lived day by day. He was a bully and perhaps in some ways he could be dishonest. At least it was in him to be dishonest if he thought dishonesty necessary. Lige *could* compromise.

Buck wondered if perhaps Lige hadn't encouraged Micah in outlawry. Someone would have to, because young Micah did not have it in him to be vicious. He was not a killer or inherently a thief. Something or someone had driven him to rob that stage.

Buck smiled to himself. He was jumping to conclusions. He

had nothing at all except a careless statement casually spoken by a disinterested Apache cowboy to sponsor the belief Micah Pheeters was the outlaw.

But an experienced manhunter actually had an inbred sensitivity to things. He'd studied Micah before the fight and afterward. He knew as surely as he knew anything that young Micah was capable of riding hard over the Pinals, robbing that Great Western stage of $15,000, and riding back in the darkest night. He knew it because that inherent sixth sense told him it was entirely possible.

But, as he came within sighting distance of the buildings he knew belonged to Franklyn Connell, he also knew Micah would not have undertaken that punishing ordeal simply for himself, or to prove his manhood. Something or someone had goaded him to it.

He clung to the belief that this someone might be sneering Lige until, with a square of orange lamp glow piercing the onward night from a front room of the Connell place, it began to dawn on him that perhaps it wasn't Lige. Perhaps it was this girl up here who Tick had also casually mentioned, this Jennie Connell.

He halted out a half mile when a dog up among the ranch buildings began to bark. Franklyn Connell's corrals were full of cattle. When that dog started tonguing, those cattle, stirred by this racket into restless wakefulness, began distantly to low. Buck went onward a quarter mile and stopped again. He saw a house door open, a man step out where that warm orange glow fell outward into the night, and step beyond the light, striding off toward some corrals. He also saw, by that same puddling light where a saddled horse stood drowsing patiently, tied to a stud ring in a hitching post. He couldn't be certain but that horse with its shaggy mane and leggy greyhound build reminded him of a horse he'd seen earlier this day. The horse young Micah had been riding.

Buck dismounted, stood by his mount's head to pinch off any nicker the animal might make if it scented the animal on ahead, and watched that man up there hike back to the house from the corral area. The man halted once. Buck heard him call the dog a name and order the dog to shut up. The dog went quiet and the man passed on back inside.

One thing was sure. That man hadn't been young Micah Pheeters. He hadn't in fact been any of the Pheeters men. He was taller than old Buster but not as tall as either Micah or Lige. Buck was satisfied, if his information was correct and Connell had only that one child, a girl, that he'd just seen Franklyn Connell himself. He got back astride, thoughtfully turned, and began a casual roundabout tour of Connell's range. He found a few cattle, mostly old bone-back cows or springy heifers, and concluded that Connell was readying a cattle drive. It did not seem at all likely Connell would try to push that many critters southward onto Matador range, so he assumed Connell was going to head for Tucson.

He ended his tour of the Connell range and struck out southerly again. He had traveled almost a mile with his thoughts and the nighttime hush, when he heard a horse coming on in a long lope behind him. He drew off westward, meaning to elude this rider, yet he did not wish to be so far out he might not catch a glimpse. He was experienced at this, and the traveler had no inkling he was not quite alone, so Buck got a good look at him in the faintly lit night. It was young Micah.

Buck let Pheeters get well ahead before cutting across his back trail, angling off southeasterly, back toward the cow camp, and listening to those rushing hoof beats die out in the quiet night. He traveled nearly another full mile before, without any warning whatsoever, a mounted man loomed up, dead ahead. Obviously this rider was not taken by surprise as Buck was. He sat there, without saying a word but with his hat brim shadowing a face set squarely toward Buck. Both this man's hands were in sight upon his saddle horn and he was not tall like Micah. In fact, at first sight, Buck thought he had encountered Tick and that the Apache had followed him after all. But that other man spoke, and his unmistakable rasping voice jarred Buck's memory hard. He'd heard this voice in this same tone not more than six hours before. It belonged to Buster Pheeters.

"You get around, don't you, Windsor?" the bleak-faced cowman said. "What you trailin' my boy for?"

"I wasn't trailing him," replied Buck truthfully.

"Then why'd you ride off when you heard him comin'?"

Buck's astonishment passed. It was replaced with disgust and irritation, both directed at himself for allowing this wizened old rattlesnake of a man to catch him off guard like this.

"I didn't know it was your son back there, but even if I had, I don't make a practice of taking chances. I'd have sloped off until I saw who it was, the same as you'd have done, Pheeters."

"All right. But what you doin' ridin' around here in the night? Too dark to find strays, Windsor, or was you interested in just Matador beef?"

This innuendo brought a bitter smile to Buck's eyes that Buster Pheeters couldn't have seen in the dark and across the distance separating them.

"With beef worth a cartwheel a head, Pheeters," he retorted, "no one'd bother stealing them. I was riding up here because I felt like it." Buck nudged his mount up a little closer to Pheeters. "Maybe you were riding around here for the same purpose."

"I got business on Perdition Range, Windsor. You ain't."

"What kind of business? Spying on Micah?"

Pheeters's fingers closed hard down over his saddle horn but that was the only detectable sign he gave that Buck had scored with his words.

"You're goin' to get killed one of these days, Windsor. You keep on chousin' folks and sneakin' around in the night and someone's goin' to give you a third eye socket."

"Not from in front they won't, Pheeters."

"I could've, right here tonight, if I'd had a mind to."

Buck wagged his head across at the smaller, older man. "Naw. You're not the dry-gulching kind. You'd call out to a man first, Pheeters."

For a full minute those two glared across without saying anything more, then Buck reined off and rode away. He did not once look back but he had the feeling up between his shoulders that Buster Pheeters was staring perplexedly, suspiciously after him. That sensation lasted almost until someone southward and on ahead made a night bird's drowsy whistle, and Buck reached up, pushed back his hat, and quietly swore at the thin old moon.

"Come on up, you sneaking Injun!" he called, still looking at the overhead sky. "This country's got more folks traveling it in the night than it has in the daytime."

Tick rode forth from the southerly gloom. He was grinning widely. His teeth shone in their startling way out of the mahogany of his pockmarked face.

"You gave old Pheeters more credit than I'd have given him, turning your back and riding off like that."

"You were covering me," stated Buck.

Tick's grin turned wicked now. "Yeah, but you didn't know it, white man. I been covering you ever since you rose up and sneaked off."

"They teach you to stick your beak into other folk's business in those mission schools, Tick?"

"No, that comes naturally. Didn't I tell you . . . I'm a lousy Apache Injun. Hell, ask Pheeters, he'll tell you we're all sneaks and thieves and murderers."

"I don't like Pheeters," said Buck. "I'll have to ask someone else. Micah maybe."

Tick's smile dwindled. His black, beady eyes drew out narrow. "Is it Micah you want? I thought it might be Lige."

"All I wanted was a little fresh air and an idea of how the Perdition Range lay."

Tick's skeptical gaze didn't waver. "In the dark," he said, "without a big moon or even any worthwhile stars?" He shook his head. "Just tell me it's none of my business, Buck. That's all right with me."

"Then why did you follow me?"

"I had a couple of ideas. I've known you one day. I've seen how fast you are with a gun. I know how you can kill a man with your fists. You're no ordinary cowboy. So, I wanted to know . . . are you here for stealing Matador cattle or to kill a man."

"You heard what I told Pheeters. With cattle bringing maybe a cartwheel a head who'd want to steal them?"

"Maybe five hundred head would make it worthwhile," murmured Tick. He shook his head, still keeping that slit-eyed stare upon Buck. "But that's not it. You don't want cattle, so it's got to be a man."

Buck reined up when the tumbled boulders where their cow camp was loomed dead ahead in the milky night. He got down, off-saddled, then turned and watched Tick care for his horse. The Apache had his back turned. He worked in that position with a deliberateness that did not escape Buck. People said Indians could read a man's soul, said they scented treachery, and never turned their backs on those in whom treachery was inherent. If this were so, then Tick was showing Buck mutely and eloquently that he trusted him. Buck grinned, tossed down his hat, and dropped beside his saddle.

"All right Tick," he said. "It's a man. But I don't know who he is."

The Apache turned, sat down, crossed-legged, and vigorously scratched his head. "Why?" he asked.

"Robbery."

"You're a lawman?"

"Arizona Ranger."

Tick showed no astonishment although he must have been surprised. He stopped scratching his head, leaned back upon his saddle, and stared over at Buck, saying nothing for a long while. Finally he bobbed his head up and down as though reconciled.

"I knew you weren't an ordinary cowboy. I knew it when you got the drop on me, when you whipped big Lige Pheeters. I also knew it when you almost jumped Tom Douglas. I think maybe Tom and Cuff guessed you weren't a run-of-the mill rider, too. It was in their eyes when they looked at you." Tick made a slow, slow smile. "You see, white man, damned Injuns read signs. They look past a man's expression."

Buck grinned back. "All right, damned Injun, just do me one more favor. Say nothing to anyone."

Tick nodded, said nothing, and lay back and closed his eyes.

Chapter Eight

Tick rode west the following day to patrol Matador grass and look out for Matador cattle. Buck rode northwest. Where they parted, the Apache put that sly gaze on Buck and said: "Don't get careless again. Lige won't forget what you did to him. Neither will old Buster."

Buck nodded. "When a man makes the same mistake twice, he deserves whatever happens to him. I'll watch."

The morning was crystal clear and pleasant. As far as Buck could see Perdition Range ran westerly and northerly to a far-off merging with the horizon. There were mountains, saw-toothed and seeming inhospitable that bent around toward the flowing southward range, but distance blurred them, made them hazy as though from a distant fire.

Buck had the suspicion of an idea. He had to verify or discard the idea that young Micah Pheeters might have that $15,000 someone had taken from the Lordsburg coach. Aside from Micah himself, and conceivably old Buster, there were two people Micah might confide in. Lige, or perhaps this Jennie Connell he supposedly was infatuated with.

But a man could hardly ride up and ask either of those people without bringing a storm down around his ears, so Buck rode leisurely along toward the Connell place. When he eventually got there, he took a patient position near a shielding land swell and watched the ranch.

That same man he'd seen by lamplight the night before was

shoeing a horse in front of the barn. There was a scarred wagon parked nearby and a girl was lashing canvas over the bows. Even from that distance Buck could make out that this girl was unmistakably female. She had dark auburn hair that caught hot sunlight and turned it back burnished and rusty-red. The high, large swell of her upper body sang across the distance to Buck, reminding him how long he'd been away from the companionship of women. He watched her from beyond the land swell, concealed from the sight of Franklyn Connell and his daughter, wondering if she returned Micah Pheeters's interest and thinking that, if she did, she must be younger than she looked from that distance.

The man straightened up from his shoeing, crossed to a gourd at the water trough, drank deeply, and flung off sweat. His faded work shirt was dark and limp where perspiration molded it to him. He was graying over the ears. His face was lean and lantern-jawed with layers of bronze coloring darkening it, and in build he was sinewy, without an ounce of surplus weight on him anywhere. He said something to the girl. She stepped around to answer back and the shape of her sang over the distance again to Buck in his hiding place.

She took the freshly shod horse, rigged it out, and mounted. Franklyn Connell ambled into the barn, came out leading another animal, tied this beast, and, with a casual wave at the departing girl, bent over and grasped a hoof.

Buck waited no longer. He wanted to meet that girl. He'd wanted to meet her even before the pull of her had sung over that separating distance to him, but now his curiosity and interest drove him to mount up and ride off with a greater determination.

She lingered a moment over at the Connell house. This gave Buck sufficient time to get well away from the ranch southward before he secreted himself athwart her suspected route, and waited. When he saw her spin out of the yard, heading south by east, he breathed a sigh of relief. If she'd headed west, he could have intercepted her, but not with the deceptive inadvertence he could use now in crossing her path.

There was a bosque of cottonwood trees between the Connell and Pheeters places. It seemed once to have shaded another ranch, but all that remained now of those buildings were rotting, charred remnants of siding and barn balks in the grass. He could imagine with no great strain what had happened here. Some family had made the fatal mistake of building a house too close to outbuildings and too distant from a water well. Apache fire arrows were made to order for situations like that, in the early days when a man was permitted just one oversight—his last one.

Buck swung in among those trees, watching the girl pass downcountry toward him. He was sure she was heading for the Pheeters place, and as he watched from within the speckled shade of that cottonwood bosque, he speculated that her father might have sent her over to ascertain whether one of the Pheeters men might not accompany them on their drive to Tucson. Of course, it would be Micah she would be going to see.

For just a detached second he felt a quick stab of fierce envy for Micah Pheeters. She was close enough now for him to see her plainly. Her features were good. In fact, she was very lovely. Her face and throat were the color of new butter. She rode with the easy, natural grace a lifelong horseman that Buck Windsor could appreciate. He was totally immersed in this physical study of her and at first did not notice that she'd altered course a little and was coming on obliquely, straight for the cottonwoods where he was motionlessly sitting his saddle. When it dawned on him that she was indeed coming right up where he was, consternation momentarily seized him. He flung around for a way out. There was none. The moment he rode out of those trees she would see him. He swung back, saw her less than a hundred yards out, stepped down quickly, picked up his mount's forefoot, and bent frowningly over it. He was caught where he had no business, without any but the most feeble excuse for being there, and for the second time within twenty-four hours had a towering feeling of anger with himself.

She came around the trees, saw him there, hauled up in an astonished slide, and dropped her reins, staring downward. He slowly raised his head, slowly dropped the horse's leg and straightened up, removing his hat as he did this. He thought his acting had to be terribly lame, terribly transparent, because the sense of being caught spying was making even the back of his neck prickle.

" 'Morning, ma'am," he said. "My horse drew up a mite lame."

She moved her tawny eyes to the horse and back again. Buck knew she'd seen through him at once because the uncooperative damned horse wasn't favoring either of his forelegs, but was standing there with his entire weight squarely upon them both. She sat still, considering him, her face blank, her eyes kindling with a skepticism as solid as it could be. She seemed not the least afraid of him but alert to his presence, curious about his identity, and why he was there on Connell range.

She wore a long tan riding skirt, a blue blouse that swelled with her breathing, and her reddish, auburn hair hung in heavy waves to her shoulders, unrestrained by a hat or even a ribbon of any kind.

"He's not lame now," she said, letting him hear that skepticism, "if he ever was, mister. Who are you? Where do you belong?"

Buck spoke his name, saying also: "I'm a Matador rider."

That skeptical look turned cool. "You're not on Matador range now," she said. She gazed steadily at him for another long moment, then spoke again. "You're the man who fought Lige Pheeters, aren't you?"

"Yes'm. News travels fast on Perdition Range."

"Bullets travel even faster, mister. You made a good enemy yesterday."

"Just one?" he asked, watching her face for a change.

"No. Buster'll remember you, too."

"Not Micah, ma'am?"

She raised one hand, brushed back a thick lock of hair, and lowered the hand again. As she tilted her head back, Buck saw the lovely turning of her throat, of her shoulders. Then she spoke gain, ignoring his question to say tartly: "There are no Matador cattle up here, Mister Windsor. What brought you?"

He tried a pleasant little gallantry. "Maybe you, ma'am. Maybe I just wanted to see if Franklyn Connell's daughter was as handsome as I'd heard."

It went over her like a passing cloud. She stared and said: "And maybe it was because you'd heard we were readying a drive to Tucson and were sent here by Tom Douglas to make certain we didn't drift any Matador beef along with our cattle."

His pleasant look faded before her increasing animosity. This wasn't going at all like he'd wanted it to. He straightened fully around toward her and dropped his reins. Filtered sunlight touched down over his rugged, strong features showing him all man. Her attention came closely upon him. Her eyes narrowed slightly in appraisal, then opened wider. When next he spoke, she listened to his voice and weighed his words. Clearly she had started out cool and skeptical and wished to remain that way. But as he spoke, he saw the change of her heavy lips, the passing quick shadow of change come to her eyes, to her expression, while she heard him out.

"No one sent me up here, but I might as well tell you I was up here last night, too. You'll hear it from Micah or old Buster sooner or later. You see, Buster caught me riding up around here in the dark. If you want to know what I was doing, I'll tell you the same as I told him. I was trying to get the lay of the range." He paused, shrugged, and went on again. "That fight with Lige . . . he brought it on, I didn't. They were on Matador land with Pheeters cattle."

"And today, right now? Your horse wasn't lame, Mister Windsor. Would you like to start over again?"

He chuckled. "I don't deserve the chance. I lied to you." He shrugged. "I saw you riding along. I got in here to watch." He shrugged again. It was not easy telling her this because she just sat up there, staring gravely down at him. She didn't make it any easier, either, with that solemn, smoothed-out expression. "That's all, I reckon. I just saw you, came in here, and watched you."

"You're new in the country, Mister Windsor. I've never seen you before."

"I haven't been in the Perdition country in a long time, Miss Connell, but I'm not exactly new hereabout."

"I thought Tick was the only Matador man riding the north country."

"I'm his pardner."

"I see. Tom Douglas doesn't think just one of his men ought to be up here among the settlers by himself. Is that it?"

"He didn't tell me that. Mind if I ask you a question now? Doesn't your paw know the bottom's dropped out of the cattle market?"

"He knows. This isn't his first drive this year."

"Well, there's not much point in a man giving his critters away, is there?"

She pursed her lips as a gust of dourness passed across her

face and disappeared. "You just ride for ranches, Mister Windsor. You wouldn't know about mortgages and things like that."

He turned, caught up his reins, mounted, and kneed his animal over in front of her. "But if he could hold on for another year the market would get better. One thing, Miss Jennie, it can't get any worse."

That gusty, dour expression came and went again. "It's not that easy. I just told you . . . there's a mortgage to be met. It must be met this year, not next year."

The conversation was going well. He levered up a look of grave concern and said: "It's none of my business. We just met and are talking, but can't your paw get a one-year extension?"

She shook her head at him.

"Well, maybe he could borrow enough to tide him over."

"Where?" she demanded bitterly. "Where can a person borrow a thousand dollars?"

Buck considered the back of one hand, turning quiet while he did this. What she had just said troubled him. She was very lovely, and if young Micah wasn't in love with her, he was a fool. Assuming he was no fool, and knowing very well Micah had visited her last night, and assuming also that she was deadly serious when she'd just now demanded where a person could borrow $1,000, then either Micah Pheeters was *not* the outlaw Buck was seeking—which made his heart sink—or else he hadn't yet told Jennie he had enough money to help her father; fifteen times more than her father needed, in fact.

"I'm sorry," he murmured. "I've seen this happen before. A person doesn't have to be kin to a loser to feel for him." He looked up. She was watching him with that feminine expression of interest again. He sighed inwardly. Jennie Connell wasn't more than sixteen years of age. He touched his hat brim and rode on out of the trees.

The thoughts of a lonely man turned often to something as desirable as Jennie Connell. Wistfulness was a sensation that frequently colored a lonely man's thinking. Once, long ago, there had been a Jennie Connell in Buck Windsor's life, but a hundred intervening campfires had come and gone since those days and now, near thirty years of age, he rode along imagining how things might have been, feeling infinitely old, infinitely alone and apart from the mainstream of his kind.

He carefully put the cameo image of young Jennie beside that other image in his secret heart and shook loose of the poignancy for a moment to consider young Micah.

If he *was* the highwayman who had robbed surly Joe Evarts's coach over near Lordsburg, then as the tool of retribution Buck Windsor was going to do more than just disrupt Micah's life. He was going to twist a knife in the heart of Jennie Connell as well, and that, he told himself as the afternoon began to soften around him, would be the meanest thing he'd ever done.

He saw a thin lift of gray smoke rising from the onward rock tumble where Tick's cow camp was. When he was a half mile closer, he also saw a saddled horse, standing in boulder shade down there that was not Tick's animal. Instantly that old inherent warning of the manhunter flashed down through him. He approached camp alert and wary.

CHAPTER NINE

Tick did not rise up from his little cooking fire or turn his head as Buck rode up, got down, and looked into the blank, considering stare of Tom Douglas. For all Tick showed, Buck might not have even been there.

Douglas inclined his head, said nothing, and watched Buck turn to unsaddling, off-bridling. There was something in the air. Buck could sense it. When he finished, he sauntered over, passed around where Tick was frying meat, squatted down, and waited. Tom Douglas was not here just because he needed a horseback ride for exercise. In his own good time he would say whatever was on his mind.

Tick looked up briefly, held Buck's glance while his back was to the scarred range boss, and somberly dropped one eyelid. Douglas came over, eased down, pushed back his hat, and reached for the coffee pot and a dented tin cup. As he poured, he said casually: "Windsor, I heard about your scrap with Lige Pheeters."

Buck raised an eyebrow at Tick, but the Apache faintly shook his head. He had not told Douglas, so it had to have reached the range boss from some other source.

"Care for some coffee?"

Buck shook his head, still silent, relaxed and waiting.

Douglas sipped, made a wry face over the strength of that black beverage, and got comfortable there in the afternoon shade.

"I don't really care that you two tangled. Not personally anyway. But I'd rather it hadn't happened."

Buck's eyes flickered over to Douglas, their glance brightening with sudden irritation. "You told Tick and me to keep outside cattle off Matador grass no matter how we had to do it," he said sharply.

Douglas didn't flare up in the face of this sudden hostility. He simply looked into the cup he was holding, squinted up his eyes, and said calmly: "Yes, and I meant it just like that, too. As I said, I'm not blaming you."

"Then who is?"

"Well, no one, exactly." Douglas gave Buck look for look. "But there's something else."

"Such as?"

"Cuff Kennedy. You recollect him at the main camp? He was the gray-headed. . . ."

"I remember him," interrupted Buck. He also remembered something else as well—Kennedy's notion that he'd seen Buck somewhere before. As he sat now, watching the elaborately casual way Tom Douglas was acting, he thought he knew what was coming next.

"Cuff sent me a note last night by one of his men from down along the border."

"It concerned me?"

"Yeah. I won't tell you what was in the note, but I'll tell you why I came up here today." Now Douglas set aside his dented cup, composed his face, and said with that hard, pale gaze of his like stone: "All I hire on, Windsor, is cowboys. If I know a feller's got trouble with the law, I don't hire him. That's been my policy for years. There's enough grief nurse-maiding five thousand and more Matador critters without buying outside trouble, too."

Buck poured himself a cup of coffee, saw Tick watching him, ignored this, and wished Douglas would get to the point. As he leaned back again, the range boss went on speaking.

"Maybe you and the law met head-on sometime. Maybe you didn't. You told me the law didn't want you. I'm taking your word for that. But now about that fight with Lige Pheeters yesterday . . . the way I heard that, you beat the hell out of him."

Buck's patience ran out. He put the coffee cup down, hard, and said to big Tom Douglas: "Why don't you just say it. Just spit it out? What's bothering you?"

"Buster Pheeters told me he thinks you're a feller who is wanted over at Raton for a couple of murders."

This time Buck and Tick exchanged a veiled look. Buck wasn't sure but he got the impression the Apache was silently laughing.

"Buster Pheeters," said Buck with strong bitterness, "saw his bullying son get larruped to a frazzle yesterday. He never saw me before that fight in his lousy lifetime, but old Buster's not one to forgive or forget. He told me that himself, after the fight. If you'd believe a man like that, then I'll just roll my blankets and hit the trail, Douglas."

"Wait a minute," said the range boss. "I said I believed you about not being wanted by the law." Douglas looked acidly over at Tick, who was dishing up food. "I pumped your pardner here." Douglas made a grunt. "Might as well talk to one of these boulders. All Tick would say was that he was there, and that Lige called you, you didn't call him."

"That's the truth."

"All right. But tell me one thing . . . if you weren't already gunning for Lige Pheeters, just why did you hammer him like that?"

Buck's eyes sprang wide open. Tom Douglas, possibly from whatever Cuff Kennedy had written him in a note, thought Buck was in the Perdition Range country because he had a grudge against Lige Pheeters. When his astonishment passed, Buck came very near to smiling.

"I never saw Lige Pheeters before yesterday in my life," he told Douglas. "And if you know any way to whip a man who's got nearly a six-inch reach on you without knocking all the fight out of him, I'd sure like to hear it. Hell, I didn't hammer him. Ask Tick there. I didn't even put him down when I could've right easily. If old Buster told you differently, he's a damned liar and he knows it."

"Will you tell me to my face that you weren't after him before you come to Perdition Range?"

"I will."

Those two rough men sat there, looking straight at one another until Tick pushed out two dented plates and said: "Eat." That one word broke the spell. The three of them ate and thought their private thoughts, and afterward had a smoke from Tom Douglas's makings. Sometime later the range boss, critically eyeing the lowering sun, stirred where he sat.

"Should be getting back," he muttered, then made no move to get up and leave. "By the way, either of you know anything about Connell making up a drive?"

"He is," stated Buck. "I saw his full corrals today."

"And last night, too," commented Douglas dryly, frowning at a ragged piece of burning cornhusk paper on his smoke.

"Buster again," growled Buck. "All right. I saw his full corrals last night, too. He's getting ready to head out for Tucson."

"He's already done that once this spring," mused Douglas, turning his thoughts to this more compelling thing and asking nothing about why Buck was riding Connell's range in the night. "Some fellers just never learn."

"He's learned," corrected Buck. "He just doesn't have any alternative."

"No? And why would that be?"

"Because he's got a mortgage payment to make."

Now both Tick and Tom Douglas sat there, gazing steadily over at Buck. They would not, either one of them, ask how he knew about this mortgage payment, because range etiquette forbade such a personal question, but they would sit as they were now sitting, and wait a long time for Buck to volunteer this interesting piece of information.

Buck let them wait. He smoked, finished his coffee, tilted his hat forward to shield both eyes from the lowering sun, and eventually told them.

"I met his daughter this morning. She told me he's got a thousand dollar mortgage payment to make, and he hasn't got the thousand, so he's going to trail over to Tucson and dump the cattle."

Douglas sat still while he ran this through his mind. Finally he drawled something that had nothing to do at all with Franklyn Connell's financial straits. He said: "She's just about the prettiest thing that ever rode down the pike, little Jennie."

"*Little* Jennie," muttered Buck. "She hasn't been *little* Jennie in three, four years."

Douglas looked up in that hard, direct way he had of skewering a man with both eyes head-on. "You and me, Windsor, we're almost old enough to be her paw."

Buck punched out his smoke, and while his head was still lowered at this occupation, he shot back a crisp answer to that. "Except that neither you nor me had the brains to be anyone's paw, Douglas. The trouble with our kind is that we use the wrong end to think with. Sitting in a saddle every day and every year may be a good way of life, but it sure proves that a man doesn't know enough to use the opposite end . . . use his head."

Tom Douglas made one of his rare grins. His knife-scarred cheek twisted tortuously from this effort but his yeasty eyes warmed to Buck. He pushed up off the ground, saying: "You win, Windsor. You got the right answers every time. Anyway, all I really wanted over here was to make sure you weren't riding some private grudge trail, weren't going to kill someone like Lige Pheeters, and get Matador into hot water."

"Now you know," stated Buck, also arising. "Anything else, boss?"

No longer smiling but with a lingering twinkle in his gaze Douglas said dryly: "Yeah, one thing. You and Tick parallel Connell's drive for a day or two and be damned sure he doesn't just accidentally have any Matador beef mixed in."

Buck nodded, walked out to Douglas's horse with him, and asked a question. "Tell me, Tom, would Connell knowingly try something like that?"

Douglas caught up his reins, fingered them for a moment, and said: "I don't think so. Not really. I don't think Buster Pheeters would, either. But it's happened, and you can guess who catches hell if our tallies come up short. Me."

"Yeah, I understand," murmured Buck. "Now, one more question. Just what did Kennedy write in that note?"

"How good is your word, Windsor?"

"Good enough. Why?"

"Give me your word you'll never say anything to Cuff and I'll tell you."

"You've got it."

"He said he'd remembered where he'd seen you. It was down in the Fort Apache country. You and another feller rode in one night, it was dark, and Cuff thought you were the feller wearing the wrist irons. Something about rustling cattle, or something like that. He didn't rightly remember."

"He sure didn't," murmured Buck, keeping a perfectly straight face because he distinctly recalled that night. It was the time he'd brought in Texas Lee Smith, a notorious outlaw, and Buck hadn't been wearing the handcuffs, it had been Smith

75

who'd been wearing them.

"Remember, Windsor, I've got your word. Cuff only thought he might be helping."

"Yeah. But if it'll make you sleep any easier, Tom, I'll also give you my word that I've never in my life stolen any cattle . . . or horses, either, for that matter."

"I'm satisfied," said Douglas. He snugged up his cinch and mounted. As he got squarely in the saddle he said: "If, when you and Tick are scouting up Connell's herd tomorrow, old Franklyn comes out all feisty about what you're doing, do us both a favor . . . don't knock hell out of him like you did with Lige. Matador gets along with these cussed settlers in the Perdition country. It doesn't take anything off 'em, but it gets along with 'em. If you get to cracking too many skulls up here, I'll have to start hiring gunslingers, and that's something I'm plumb against."

Buck nodded, stepped aside, and stood a moment after the range boss had departed, looking after him. He didn't hear Tick come up, wasn't aware of the Apache at all until Tick said: "You got to know him. Like I already told you, Douglas is a good man."

Buck turned. "Someday you're going to slip up behind me like that and I'm going to shoot you."

Tick made his slow, raffish smile, his cheeks puckered until his eyes were hidden and he drawled: "It's against the law to shoot Injuns any more, didn't you know that? In mission school a teacher showed us a copy of the Congressional ruling that says that. You want another cup of my very fine coffee?"

As they started shuffling back toward the little camp, Buck said: "Your very fine coffee would float a horseshoe with the lousy horse attached to it."

Tick said no more until they were squatting together by the dying fire, sipping the coffee, then he looked around and said:

"Tom sure pumped me before you rode up. Did he tell you what Cuff wrote him?"

"Yeah, that I was an outlaw, a cow thief."

Tick stared briefly, then threw back his head and roared. Buck waited for this extreme amusement to lessen, brushed the Apache's thick arm with his fingers, and said: "Thanks, Tick, for keeping your mouth closed."

"It was real easy, Buck. Tom was so fired up he didn't really give me a chance to say anything anyway. Good coffee, eh?"

Buck looked into his cup, looked around into that perfectly round, pockmarked, villainous, and mahogany-colored face. "What'd you put in it, dog-gone you?"

"A little juice from a few mashed-up mescal beans. Not as good as whiskey, but out here where would a feller get any whiskey?"

Buck put down his cup, said a tart word, and went over to his blankets. Mescal beans, or seed pods, when properly squeezed of their juice, had an effect upon men something like strong whiskey. If there was one thing he didn't want on the morrow, it was a hangover headache.

CHAPTER TEN

Buck did not know that Franklyn Connell was going to start his drive the following day. Tom Douglas had implied that this was to be the case though, and the longer Buck dwelt upon it the more convinced he became that when Buster Pheeters and Douglas had met, Pheeters must have told Tom that. Not that this detail of the actual drive was important, and yet Buck had seen Connell shoeing his horses, had seen Jennie securing the wagon canvas, and felt confident Pheeters was right.

But one thing kept troubling him. If Micah had that $15,000 from the stage robbery, why hadn't he offered the father of the girl he undoubtedly loved $1,000 of it?

It was this perplexing thought that kept him silent while he and Tick rode together toward the Connell Ranch by a southerly route that took them between the Pheeters place and the Connell place.

It bothered him particularly because, if Micah wasn't the highwayman he had tracked to Perdition Range, who was?

Tick raised an arm. "He got an early start."

Buck raised his eyes to look far ahead. A dust cloud lay low, off in the dazzling west. He could make out very little actually because of this distance, but there was no mistaking the lowing of cattle up ahead. With a deep frown he pushed his mount into a loose lope. Tick kept up, riding with the grace of his people. There existed nowhere on earth any better riders than Apache Indians, although almost any land had better horsemen; they

were seldom considerate of an animal while astride it, but Tick
seemed to be an exception. After a mile of hurrying over that
morning-lit, huge expanse of range, he said protestingly to Buck:
"We don't have to kill these horses, do we?"

Buck slowed, said nothing, and concentrated on peering
ahead. He could now make out a wagon. It was, he felt certain,
the same wagon that he'd seen in Connell's ranch yard the
morning before. He slowed to a steady walk and shook his head.
Something was wrong here. Either his theory concerning young
Micah was entirely in error, or, for some reason he could not
imagine, young Micah was not going to help Jennie's father.

Twenty minutes later, as he and Tick came almost even with
the drag end of those cattle shuffling along, the Apache said
Micah's name and pointed up where a point rider was slouch-
ing.

"You sure?" asked Buck. "You sure it isn't Lige or even old
Buster?"

"I'm sure," responded Tick, his wet, black eyes whipping
around, his expressionless moon face, beginning to show the
shadow of a suspicion. "It's not Lige you want, it's Micah, isn't
it?"

"Yes, it's Micah."

Suddenly, from far back, a man's high cry rang out. Both
Buck and Tick swung in their saddles, but that oncoming horseman, if he'd noticed the two Matador men at all, gave no sign
of it. He was dusting along, waving his hat at the drag rider of
Connell's ambling herd.

Buck didn't have to be told who that man was. He recognized
old Buster Pheeters without any difficulty, and reined to a halt
to watch Buster swing up parallel, then continue on past.

"Something's up," muttered Tick.

Buck made no comment. He saw Buster and Franklyn
Connell meet a short distance beyond the herd, speak back and

forth briefly, then both spin out in a long forward run for the point of the moving herd.

"He doesn't want Micah to go," said Tick, bringing Buck's attention around with this remark.

"Why not?"

Tick wagged his head, his quick, bright stare fixed northward where those riders were hurrying along, small in the distance. "There's no great admiration between Buster and Franklyn."

Buck was surprised at this. He waited for the Apache to say more and Tick obliged.

"Micah hangs around over at the Connell place too much. I know Buster doesn't like that. He doesn't want his boys to marry."

Buck, remembering the fierce look on Buster's face when he'd run on to him the night he'd spied on the Connell place, let out a soft sigh. Tick had just given him a reason for old Buster to be skulking around on the Connell range that night.

"You know that for a fact?" he demanded.

"Yeah. You can't ride Perdition Range as long as I have and not see things. Old Buster's jealous. He doesn't much care for Franklyn anyway, but since Micah's been courting Jennie, he's been like a bear with a sore behind, always growling and looking mean." Tick shook his head again. "Indians are sometimes like that, too. They got sons, they don't want women to complicate their lives."

Buck straightened around. The wagon had slowed, then halted. People were crowded around, up there. It looked to Buck as though Jennie was in the midst of whatever was being said. "Maybe this might not be a bad time to ride on up and inspect the cattle," he said.

Tick shot him a disapproving look. "It'd be the worst time," he contradicted. "Old Buster'll be mad. He's got no use for you already. Tom said not to start no wars with these people. You bust in on a big family fight and hell'll pop." Tick paused, staring far off at those people. "Just wait. Whatever happens'll bust out soon now."

Tick was right. A moment later two riders left that canvas-topped trail wagon, riding stiffly and swiftly back over the trail Connell's herd had made.

"Buster and Micah," said Buck.

Tick grunted assent to this observation, then offered an opinion of his own. "Buster won. He's taking his boy home." Tick added something uncomplimentary to this and curled his lips downward. "Indian boys get as old as Micah . . . they do what they want."

Buck tried to remember Micah's face, his eyes, and the set of his jaw. He concluded after a while that Micah hadn't appeared to him as a youth likely to be cowed easily.

"Come on," he ground out. "Let's go up to the wagon."

Tick booted out his horse beside Buck, but as they sped northward he said: "I'm getting a bad feeling. You talk to 'em, if you want. I'll cut off and ride through the cattle. I'll watch. When you leave, I'll come along."

Old Buster and his youngest son were more than a mile southeastward by the time Tick split off, heading for Connell's cattle. Buck saw them small in the distance, still riding side-by-side. This entire thing puzzled him.

When he got close to the wagon, close enough to see that he and Tick had been seen and were being studied by Franklyn Connell and Jennie, he slowed to a walk, and at this gait covered the last three hundred yards. When he halted to nod down where Connell was standing, looking grim and savage, he noticed that Jennie recognized him, turned her face from him, and climbed back to the high wagon seat to sit there all loose and distant.

"Matador," snapped Franklyn Connell. "I wondered how long it'd be before Tom sent someone after us."

Buck had never seen Connell close up before. The cowman was spare, leaned down to a rawhide toughness, and his blue gaze was frosty. Like Lige Pheeters, he was a type of man; he belonged to no other environment on earth than the one that had formed and molded him. He wore his gun as a man who was thoroughly familiar and proficient with it and its uses. Standing upon the ground now, holding the reins to his saddled horse, Franklyn Connell was tough and resourceful and ready for whatever life might throw at him, including Buck Windsor. His gaze neither wavered nor blinked; it was like a shaft of blue steel.

"You don't believe in common manners, do you?" he snapped at Buck. "You could've asked first, then sent your pardner riding through my herd."

Buck ignored that. He braced into the roiled, angry wrath of Connell and said: "Looks like you lost a cowboy."

"That any of your affair?" Connell growled. "Or is Tom Douglas loaning me two Matador men to help with my drive?"

Buck looked over the angry man's head to the wagon seat. "What happened, Miss Jennie?" he asked quietly. "Old Buster make Micah quit?"

The lovely girl nodded but neither verbally answered nor turned so Buck could see her face. Franklyn Connell said quickly, sharply: "You're getting almighty personal, cowboy. Maybe you need a lesson in manners."

Now Jennie spoke. She turned and said in a small, unsteady way: "Pa, he's Windsor. He's the one that whipped Lige."

Connell's granite stare didn't change but he said nothing more for a moment. Instead, he turned, looked out where Tick was reining back and forth through his herd, and mumbled: "There's no Matador beef here, mister. Tom Douglas knows me a sight better'n this."

"Tom Douglas didn't tell us there'd likely be Matador beef

here, Mister Connell. All he said was that sometimes strays got mixed into these drives. In fact, he told us last night you'd be the least likely to pick up Matador critters and carry 'em along."

Connell's bitter profile looked craggy the way he stood there, watching Tick. Beyond him and higher up on the wagon seat, Jennie finally looked directly over at Buck. She had control now; her face was impassive, but she'd been crying. Buck saw that in an instant. It made his rancor toward Buster Pheeters stronger. It also made him feel something very close to contempt for young Micah.

"If you hold us up much longer," she said to Buck, "we won't make first water before sunset, and the cattle'll drift all night with just the two of us to ride herd on them."

"Sure," said Buck softly. "We won't hold you up. You can leave any time you've a mind to." He and the lovely girl exchanged a long glance. "Miss Jennie, mind a sort of personal question? What could Buster say that'd pull Micah away like this?"

She regarded him steadily for a long time without speaking. It was as though she was trying to make up her mind about him, as though she was seeking some conclusion about him. He smiled a little at her.

"If I'd been Micah, believe me, Jennie, ten like old Buster couldn't drag me away from you. Not even twenty like him."

Now Franklyn Connell swung back. He said in a jarringly harsh and bitter tone: "That's what I've been saying. Micah's a damned poor excuse for a growed man, to let Buster read him off like he just did here at this wagon, without once speaking up, to let old Buster make him go back with that silly story about Lige."

Buck, annoyed by this rush of caustic criticism, said: "Keep out of this, Connell." He said it swiftly and roughly, saw Connell stiffen with surprise, and ignored that, too.

"What did Buster say, Jennie? Is it simply because he doesn't want Micah near you?"

She nodded, still keeping silent, and once again her father broke in, this time more wrathful than ever.

"What d'you mean telling me to keep out of this? Jennie's my daughter. You nor no saddle bum like you can. . . ."

"Whoa," said Buck suddenly, at this juncture recalling Franklyn Connell's former last sentence. "What silly story did old Buster tell you about Lige?"

But Franklyn Connell was a man who, once brought to total anger, did not recognize or heed interruptions or diversions.

"You Matador men have some idea you own Perdition Range. Let me tell you something, Windsor . . . and I don't give a damn if you are the man who whipped Lige Pheeters . . . I was running cattle on this range before Matador ever brought in a single herd. I was branding my beef with one hand and holding a gun in the other hand against skulking Apaches before you were born."

Buck's temper rose dangerously high. He looked down, then up again. Jennie was watching him. She seemed scarcely to hear her angry father at all. Something in the depths of her eyes seemed infinitely sad to Buck. He knew nothing of women but he *did* understand what it was like when the young and the inexperienced encounter their first genuine disillusionment in life. He was so absorbed with this train of thought he wasn't aware that Franklyn Connell was no longer speaking, not until he dropped his eyes, saw Connell's leathery, tough-set face, and heard Connell say: "If he did anything like that, then it wasn't any accident. I've known Lige Pheeters since he was born. He was a mean kid and he's a mean man."

Buck brought his thoughts back down to Connell. "What did Lige Pheeters do?" he asked.

"I just told you what Buster said, damn it."

"Tell me again."

"He found fifteen thousand dollars."

Buck sat there in total shock, staring at Franklyn Connell.

"Buster said Lige found that fifteen thousand dollars and Micah jumped on his horse and left us out here, riding like a madman. As I just told Jennie when you rode up, no decent man who'd said he loved a girl would. . . ."

Buck whipped his horse around and went racing over where Tick was sitting, waiting for him. Behind him Franklyn Connell and his daughter stared, utterly dumbfounded.

CHAPTER ELEVEN

Buck ran his horse past Tick, calling to him: "Head for the Pheeters place! Come on!"

Tick obeyed, booting his mount over into a belly-down run. He made no attempt to call out a question. He simply rode swiftly behind Buck and did not slow until, a half mile from the Pheeters' buildings, Buck slowed. Then Tick pushed on up, looked ahead, and looked back.

"What the hell?" he said, just that and nothing more.

Buck, concentrating on those silent, forbidding buildings ahead, made no reply for a long while. He saw no sign of horses, no indication that old Buster and his sons were anywhere around, and yet he was not anxious to rush into the yard.

Eventually he dismounted, tossed Tick his reins, and snaked out his booted carbine. "Stay with the horses," he ordered. "If a fight starts, I'll come back . . . don't you come in."

He went ahead with a great stillness all around him, got in close behind the barn, harkened there for horse sounds, heard none, and jumped around the door to land crouched. Nothing happened. He straightened up, walked forward toward the yonder ranch yard, and while he was doing this he looked right and left. The barn was empty; no saddled horses were in it. In fact, there weren't even any stalled horses.

Out in the sun-lashed yard there was nothing to see, either. He stepped out into plain sight, convinced now that old Buster and young Micah had not returned here. Convinced that if

86

what Franklyn Connell had told him was true about Lige's finding that $15,000, that Lige, if he'd found it secreted at the ranch, had taken it and gone.

That worried him. Lige knew Perdition Range better than Buck did. With a head start Lige could possibly get entirely out of the country with Jim Evarts's money.

He grounded his carbine, stared over at the house, swung, and whistled to catch Tick's attention. When the Apache swung forward in response to that whistle, Buck flagged him on in. Tick started forward at once, riding his own horse and leading Buck's mount.

Buck started on over the yard toward the main house. He was on the porch waiting, when Tick arrived, tossed over his reins, and stepped down to lash both horses to a rack.

"You ain't going to break into the house, are you?" Tick asked, looking doubtful about all this.

Buck said—"I've got to."—and raised a thick leg and violently kicked the door. It broke loose and shivered inward. Tick, standing by their animals, looked worried. He kept swinging his head from side to side, looking here and there. He did not follow Buck into the Pheeters house, which was just as well because after only a few moments Buck strode back out again. He was still holding his Winchester, but now he was also holding an empty pair of worn old saddlebags.

With a bitter word Buck tossed the saddlebags over into the dust near Tick. He walked out, stepped over those bags, and held out his open palm. There, lying limply across his hand, was a crisp new $20 bill.

"All that's left of fifteen thousand," he said to the Apache.

Tick looked down, looked up, and softly shook his head. "Stolen money?"

Buck pocketed the bill, went over to push his carbine into its boot, and step up over leather, then he answered: "Yeah, that fifteen thousand was robbed off a Great Western coach over near Lordsburg last week."

Tick re-mounted, his face assuming a look of gradual comprehension. "And you trailed the outlaw here," he mused, piecing all this together, "and when I found you, it was no accident."

"No accident at all." Buck turned his animal, ran a long thoughtful gaze over the empty countryside, and swore with strong feeling. "We should've followed Micah and Buster."

"We didn't know, then," stated Tick. He came over beside Buck, hung his head in a frowning way, seemed to be still putting pieces to this puzzle together in his mind and eventually said: "But why Micah? Lige'd be a much better bet. He's ornery and. . . ."

"Because you told me about seeing Micah coming home in the small hours, Tick, and that just happened to be the right direction for the highwayman I was trailing."

Tick's eyes cleared a little. He began carefully to study Buck. "Where were the saddlebags hid?"

"In Micah's bedroom, a lean-to built on the back of the damned house. Hid under the floor. The board was still lying where Lige left it after yanking it up."

"How would Lige know where to look?"

Buck shrugged. "He knew. Right now that's not bothering me. When kids grow up together, they know each other's secret places. Maybe Lige was suspicious. Maybe Micah said something to make him suspicious. I don't know. I *do* know Lige found that money under the floor in Micah's room, and now he's making a run with it." Buck removed his hat, swiped at forehead sweat, crushed the hat back on, and said: "But where? Buster and Micah evidently knew, but they've gone, too, which leaves me in a hell of a pickle."

Tick was unperturbed. "Naw," he grunted. "That'll be no

problem. You want 'em, come on, we'll go find 'em."

Tick led off out of the yard in a long lope. He never once looked back to make certain Buck was following. Instead, he kept swinging his head from side to side. He evidently did not really expect to see any of the Pheeters men, but until he got northward nearly two miles he kept swiveling right and left anyway, because until he got up where Buster and Micah had passed along, he had nothing else to do.

But when Tick stopped and pointed earthward, his interest narrowed down considerably. He was absorbed now only in those fresh horse tracks below and in front. "That's Micah and his paw," he told Buck. "See how they're digging in . . . those tracks. Buster and Micah are riding hard. Men don't go that fast in hot weather unless they got a reason."

"Yeah, like Lige."

Tick nodded, turned, and began jogging along parallel to those dug-in, shod-horse marks in the tough short grass. He was not the least bit excited. In fact, when he spoke, his voice was almost drowsy.

"If a man knows who he's after, he can sometimes guess ahead and get around him. But I don't know Lige that well. Even if I did, I wouldn't try it with him. He's not a simple man. He's treacherous and sly and . . . well, like the old-time Apache raiders."

"You're doing fine," said Buck. "Just keep it up."

Tick squinted skyward, shrugged at the sun, and looked back downward. "We'll find them. Maybe they'll split up, maybe they'll get into a fight over all that money, but we'll find 'em. You know what tracking a man is, Buck . . . it's never quitting, never hurrying, and never stopping. When I was a kid, we used to track antelope like this. Sure, any antelope, even a sick one, can outrun a man or a horse. But he can't outlast a man, so that's how you eventually get him."

Tick covered nearly two miles before those tracks changed course, turned due southward. He frowned a little over this. Buck knew what he was doing. Tick, who knew Perdition Range and the desert beyond like a book, was puzzling out what Micah and Buster had in mind. He was trying to anticipate their thoughts, and hence their actions.

When the sun reached its overhead hottest intensity, hung there a while, then listed off to one side slightly, Tick said: "I'm not so sure they know where Lige went. I think they're trying to ride from north to south so maybe they'll cut his sign."

Buck had another thought. Mexico was southward and he said so, but Tick shook his head about this. "I don't think Lige'll try for the border. It's too far. Cuff Kennedy's down there with his Matador crew, and Lige only has one horse, which ain't enough horseflesh because he'll run out of grass range pretty soon and have eighty miles of pure desert to cross. Naw, I think he'll either circle back and head for Tucson, or keep east and head for one of the Arizona towns. Lordsburg maybe."

As Tick finished saying this, he looked up. He seemed to be balancing something in his mind, but when he didn't say it, Buck prompted him.

"You got an idea?"

"Yeah, but not a very good one. I was just wondering if maybe one of us hadn't ought to head for a butte somewhere and get atop it. On a clear day like this you can see a rider's dust for twenty-five miles." Then Tick wagged his head and voiced the objection that had occurred to him. "But the hell of that is there are only two of us. If there were ten, it'd be different. The old-timers used to put a scout atop a butte and he'd signal 'em with a piece of polished steel. Two flashes meant they should bear right, three flashes bear left. One flash, straight ahead. They could run down a man they couldn't see that way, real easy. But with us, it wouldn't work too well."

"You figure they'll put up a fight?"

Tick looked caustically over at Buck. "Wouldn't you, for fifteen thousand dollars?"

Buck didn't answer. He kept remembering the surly, treacherous look of big Lige Pheeters.

They came onto a bunch of Matador cows with calves. Tick screwed up his face. "If they're smart, they'll let those damned critters hide their tracks."

Buck hoped the Pheeterses weren't smart, and as it turned out they weren't. The tracks suddenly swung westerly.

Tick grunted. "The big circle," he muttered. "If we'd been able to see ahead, we'd have saved ourselves a heap of saddlebacking. Micah and old Buster made all these tracks on purpose, I think. They're *coyote*. They figure someone might follow 'em, so, to give themselves time, they did all this riding to throw us off, maybe lose us, or at least hold us up until they can get to Lige."

Buck had a different idea. He still did not believe old Buster Pheeters would condone outlawry, particularly by one of his own sons. He thought, instead, that Tick's earlier notion was nearer correct—Micah and his father were making a huge quartering ride to intercept Lige, and now, having combed the southward range without encountering him, were swinging back west. He thought they would eventually also swing northward again, too, heading back up toward their ranch.

A half hour later the tracks turned exactly as Buck had thought they might. Now Tick reversed his opinion, too, saying the Pheeterses were heading for their home country again. He also was beginning to weary of all this slow-pacing beneath a punishing springtime sun.

"Let's take a chance and forget the tracks for a while. Let's head on up to the Pheeters place. If we don't find 'em, we can always quarter, pick up the sign, and track 'em again."

They did that, riding at an easy lope for a long time, rarely saying anything to one another, feeling the piled up intensity of early afternoon heat around them as they grimly, doggedly persevered.

When the Pheeters Ranch buildings showed on ahead, Buck suddenly saw several riders far off moving northwest, in the direction Franklyn Connell had taken with his cattle drive. He speculated on this, wondered if perhaps Lige hadn't joined his father and brother after all, and all of them were now rushing to overtake Connell. Why they would do this escaped him; in fact, he didn't think it made much sense. Still, his two previous hunches had proven correct, so this one might also turn out to be right.

They were slightly over a mile from the Pheeters buildings, with those onward horsemen beginning to fade out through distant heat haze, when Tick slowed to a walk, crossed both hands upon his saddle horn, and said, squinting far ahead: "Who the hell is that up there?"

"Pheeters?" asked Buck, scarcely able to make out those horsemen.

"Naw, there are five of 'em. Even if Buster and his boys got friends all of a sudden, who would they be? Outside of Connell there's no one else lives hereabout."

Buck booted his animal over into a lope again, rushing up toward the ranch buildings. Behind him the Apache cowboy parted his lips, blew out a resigned breath, and followed after. He was still as calm and detached as he'd been right from the start.

Chapter Twelve

Two horsemen had been at the ranch. Buck read their sign with no difficulty even before Tick got up where he'd stopped near the house. Those two riders had also changed horses, which made Buck inwardly groan. They'd left two sweaty, ridden-down animals in a corral behind the barn, had rigged out two fresh beasts, and had gone on.

"Micah and his paw," surmised the Apache. "But they still don't know where Lige went."

Buck, remembering that Franklyn Connell had a small remuda of loose stock with his drive, only casually glanced over at the house as he said: "Come on. There are no more horses here. Let's go borrow a couple from Connell."

Tick shrugged. He, too, was gazing toward the house, toward that broken door hanging upon one hinge. "Something's wrong here," he murmured. "We saw five riders, not two, and yet two riders have been here." Tick swung to begin a systematic examination of the ground roundabout.

Buck, puzzled now, also studied the yard for additional tracks. He found none and neither did Tick, so he said: "Let's head after those five riders. They were headed for Connell's drive."

Tick obeyed, but shook his head perplexedly as they rode northward out of the ranch yard. "Something's wrong," he muttered again.

They rode for a long hour before coming within sight of Franklyn Connell's wagon and cattle. The wagon was not moving and the cattle had drifted, fanning out in all directions to graze. As he approached, Buck faintly frowned. At first there was no sign of anyone up there, with the wagon, and those horsemen, whoever they had been, were no longer anywhere in sight. Buck wrinkled his nose, turned and shot a quick look at the Apache. Tick returned this look but said nothing.

They were within fifty feet of the wagon before both of them simultaneously saw, and heard, the rasping scrape of steel over wood. Without a word Tick dropped from his saddle like a stone. Buck did the same, for although he hadn't sighted that gun barrel he knew the sound of a weapon being pushed over a wagon's side. He spotted the barrel just as he struck down. It was canting downward from between wagon box and canvas, its holder hidden completely from view. Buck rolled frantically and flashed a groping right hand for his six-gun. He got his weapon palmed and brought to bear, but that rifleman inside the wagon did not fire.

It was a bad ten seconds before the rifle barrel swung aimlessly, tilting skyward, and Buck realized that whoever was inside Connell's wagon wasn't going to shoot.

He rolled his head, seeking the Apache. Tick was there, belly-down and slit-eyed, his six-gun up and also cocked. Tick seemed to blend with the earth. As Buck watched, he made a slow faint scowl, his tongue darted out, darted in, and Tick switched his attention the slightest bit to look squarely at Buck.

The wait was seemingly endless. There was not a sound to be heard anywhere around. Buck got up to one knee, hung there watching that tilted rifle barrel, then stood up. He took several tentative, onward steps, got to the wagon's fore wheel, draped a booted foot upon the hub, and twisted from the waist to motion with his gun hand for Tick to go around the back, go around by the tailgate.

That was when they both heard the groan.

Buck yanked straight around, hesitated for just one small moment, then lunged upward, caught the high overhead seat, and straightened up with his left hand brushing aside the wagon canvas so he could see in.

Tick, watching him from near the wagon's rear wheel, saw Buck slowly holster his weapon, slowly step over the wagon seat, and disappear beyond the canvas. Tick went on around back, lifted the canvas there, and peered in. A man was lying limply sprawled beside that canted Winchester. He was face down but Tick knew him at once. It was wispy Buster Pheeters.

"Climb on in," said Buck, as he got down beside the cowman, gently rolled Pheeters over, and gazed steadily at the gunshot wound in Pheeters's side.

Tick grunted up and over the tailgate. "Been shot?" he queried.

"Yeah, in the side. Doesn't look very nice with all the blood, but I'd guess it's not too serious. Maybe two, three busted ribs."

Tick came up, squatted down, and peered into the unconscious cowman's face. He wagged his head back and forth. "Fifteen thousand dollars is a lot of money, but it wouldn't do anyone any good if they're dead." He looked up. "Lige, you reckon?"

Buck put both hands palms upward. "Maybe. But what was old Buster doing here, who were those riders we saw, and where is everyone now? Tick, this thing keeps getting more complicated as time passes."

"And it's passing," muttered the Indian, soberly regarding Buster Pheeters. "Afternoon'll be gone in another three hours. After that . . . what? Can't track 'em in the dark."

"Yeah," muttered Buck, straightening back. "Hand me a dipper full of that water from the bucket." As he waited for Tick to comply, he said: "Where's Connell? Where's Jennie? Dammit,

Tick, I think there's more to this than just fifteen thousand dollars."

Tick handed over the dipper full of water and watched Buck bring Buster Pheeters around. Together they worked over the injured man, caring for his bullet wound, propping him up, and making him as comfortable as they could.

Pheeters was pale under his sun-layered bronze coloring. It took several minutes for his eyes to focus fully. He saw Buck but watched Tick more closely, his expression wire-tight with pain, his lips sucked flat over his teeth, and his fists clenched.

"Who shot you?" Buck asked.

Pheeters's eyes swiveled to Buck's face but he said nothing. There was a roiled sort of movement in the depths of his eyes as though he might be forcing himself back to full rationality.

"Where's Lige?" Buck asked. "What happened here? Where's Micah and Jennie and old Connell?"

Pheeters laboriously worked his lips forming words, struggling through shock to utter them. "Never saw Franklyn . . . or Jennie. Just saw . . . them. . . ."

"Them?"

"Two riders, leavin' our ranch . . . then a third one, far out . . . watchin'. They . . . broke into the house. They . . . broke into the house. They . . . robbed the place."

Buck looked at Tick. The Indian was looking more perplexed than ever. He made a circling motion at the side of his temple with one finger, then lowered it to point at Buster Pheeters. Buck understood what Tick meant but shook his head. Pheeters wasn't out of his mind; he was positive of that. He turned back to his questioning again.

"Outlaws," gasped Pheeters. "Three . . . outlaws, Micah and I was lookin' for Lige's sign. Couldn't find Lige. Saw those men . . . thought Lige might be with them. Rushed up. They fired . . . hit me. Chased me 'n' Micah here . . . to Connell's wagon

. . . left me for dead and rode off. . . ."

"Rode off with Micah?"

Pheeters weakly inclined his head. He licked his lips and started to form more words. Buck put up a hand. "Save your breath," he murmured. "You're pretty well shot up. Save your strength until later."

Pheeters's lips formed an unmistakable word: "Bad?"

Buck chose his reply to this carefully. "Busted ribs and you've lost considerable blood, but if you lie still and keep those bandages Tick and I've wrapped around you in place, you'll make it all right."

Buck and old Pheeters exchanged a long, long look. There was much to be asked and answered between them. Buck caught Tick's eye and jerked his head sideward. The two of them got carefully back down out of Connell's wagon, came together over by their horses, and stood for a second or two considering one another in wry bewilderment.

"Three outlaws passing through," said Buck. "That's the way I understand it. Buster and Micah saw them at the ranch, thought maybe they might be Lige with a couple of friends, and rushed them. The outlaws of course thought Micah and his paw were coming out to do battle, so they fired on 'em and drilled old Buster."

"Where's Micah, then?" asked the Apache, wrinkling his forehead. "I tell you this thing was mixed up enough before, but now it's a real mess. And where's Lige with all that money?"

"I think that's probably what the outlaws also want to know. Maybe old Buster said something they heard while he was out of his mind. If that's so, Tick, they'd know damned well old Buster was beyond telling them anything. . . ."

"So they took Micah along with them," broke in the Apache, his face beginning to clear.

"Yeah, but I don't think Micah has any more idea where Lige

is than we do. If he had, or if his paw had, they'd have rushed to Lige. They wouldn't have done all that other riding."

Tick agreed with this. He turned and ran his black gaze along the ground to where a number of horsemen had briefly halted, then hurried on. He followed out those tracks, gradually lifting his head as he did that, until the tracks were beyond his immediate sighting. "We'll get them," he murmured to Buck. "Like I told you before, we just keep going and eventually we come on to them."

Buck, however, did not see their predicament as being that simple. If they abandoned Buster Pheeters and he became delirious again, began threshing around and opened his wound, he could easily bleed to death. Also, there was the possibility that. . . .

Three distant gunshots, ringing out, shattered Buck's thoughts, brought him up stiffly, and whirling toward the distant west.

"Pistols," he snapped.

Tick lunged for his horse, sprang up, and gathered his reins. "Connell," he spat out. "They come onto the Connells out there with the cattle somewhere."

This was in Buck's view entirely possible. He had a hard decision to make, but he made it thinking of Jennie in the hands of three fierce, hard-riding, transient outlaws of this desert country. He knew the kind those men undoubtedly were, had spent years fighting against their kind. He'd also seen what they did to beautiful young girls and lonely cowmen caught off guard out with their herds. He dug in the spurs and went plunging along behind Tick, hoping Buster Pheeters would cling to rationality until he could get help for him.

Tick sighted something and flagged onward with his thick, stubby right arm. Buck kneed his horse up closer and followed out the direction in which Tick was pointing. The Apache called out: "Two downed horses with people forted up behind 'em!"

Buck made this out, swung his head, and saw several riders disappearing around the base of a long, broad land swell. This was only a fleeting sighting he had, and afterward, when a cry rang out over where those two dead horses lay, he forgot for the time being about those riders to rush up with Tick and slide to a halt where Jennie Connell was staring out at them from an ashen face. Buck could see her lips move seconds before words came out. He left his horse and crossed over to her in several long strides, then he saw what she'd been trying to tell him. Her father was behind one of those shot horses, lying face down and completely quiet.

Tick had paused long enough to fetch along his carbine. From time to time he threw a rearward look over where those riders had flashed out of sight behind the land swell.

Franklyn Connell had been shot twice, once through the right shoulder and once through the right hip. He'd also been creased by a slug that had laid the side of his scalp open. It was this wound that had stretched him out face down and unconscious.

Buck went to work making bandages. He only looked up once at Jennie. She was sitting beside him, watching her father dry-eyed and seemingly breathless, as though shock held her firmly.

He said to her: "What happened?"

"We were . . . trying to gather the strays," she whispered. "I didn't see them coming until. . . ."

"Until one of them fired," guessed Buck, positioning his wide shoulders so that Jennie couldn't see his bloody hands at work upon her father.

"Yes, until someone fired a gun. Then my father cried out to me and fell off his horse. There were four of them. I'm sure . . . I saw Micah with them. . . ."

"You did, but he's their prisoner, Jennie, he wasn't one of them. His paw's back at your wagon, also shot."

"But . . . but who are they? What do they want?"

Buck let that question go unanswered as he beckoned for Tick to help him ease the unconscious man up against a dead horse. "Hold his neck," he told the Apache, "while I wrap something around his head." Tick kneeled to comply.

"Jennie," said Buck, "I want you to listen carefully to what I'm going to tell you. I want you to take my horse and ride hard for the Matador camp south of here. Don't stop until you get there. Find Tom Douglas, tell him what's happened up here, and that we need help. Then get a fresh horse and lead the Matador men back here. They'll have to track us, but after it gets dark, tell them we'll try to set a fire, or fire a shot now and then. Jennie, do you understand?"

"Yes," she said in a faint, small voice.

"Can you make it?"

"Yes," she said again, arising up off the ground.

"Then go on."

CHAPTER THIRTEEN

For a moment Tick and Buck watched the girl ride off southward before finishing with her father. Once, Franklyn Connell groaned. Buck looked around for a canteen, found none, and looked back to find Tick holding out a tobacco sack with unmistakable meaning. Buck twisted up a smoke, lit it, and blew several clouds into Franklyn Connell's face. It didn't work as well at rousing the injured man as that dipper of water had worked upon Buster Pheeters, but it did work. Connell opened his eyes, choked, coughed, and flinched.

Buck identified himself, waited a moment, then asked the wounded man what had happened. Connell had trouble remembering. He gritted his teeth against the throbbing pain inside his skull and his eyes copiously watered. Suddenly then, with entire clarity, he looked up, his gaze large and frantic.

"Jennie," he choked out. "Where's Jennie?"

"She's all right," Buck replied. "I sent her for help. Now listen to me, Connell. Tick and I are going after the men who did this. While you're alone here, don't move or. . . ."

"That damned rotten Micah Pheeters," ground out the injured man, breaking in with his harshness and his anger. "I saw him with them plain as day. That dirty rotten son-of-a-bitch."

"Hold it, Connell," said Buck sharply. "Micah was their prisoner. His paw's back at your wagon with a gunshot wound in his side. Tick and I were patching him up when we heard the firing over here."

Connell moaned, put up a hand to his head, and said in a rough gasp: "I got hit . . . in the head."

"Yes, but it was a crease. You also got hit in the hip and the arm, so just sit easy and don't move. You hear me?"

"I heard you. Where is . . . Jennie?"

"I told you. I sent her for help. Listen to me, Connell. Don't move or you'll start the bleeding all over again. Sit right still until help comes."

"I will," said the injured man. "But . . . why? Who were they and why'd they open up on us? We were . . . only rounding up some strays."

"They're renegade outlaws, Connell. They kill for any reason . . . for money, for fresh horses. Sometimes they kill so no witnesses are left around. Don't worry about that right now. You'll make it, and Jennie's safe. Just sit still right where you are and be quiet. All right?"

"Yes. All right, Windsor. I'm . . . obliged to you. To both of you."

Buck stood up. Across from him Tick also came upright off the ground. The Indian's gaze was somber. "What about Lige?" he asked. "He's not with that bunch that's got Micah."

Buck's brows drew inward and downward. Tick had put his finger squarely upon what was now beginning to bother him. He of course couldn't have left Pheeters and Connell without doing what he could for them both, but Micah was a different matter. He'd come to Perdition Range to apprehend a stage robber and retrieve that stolen $15,000. Micah no longer had that money. His brother had it. The question that bothered Buck now was the dilemma of his duty. He should concentrate on finding that money. As for Micah, who he was satisfied now was the actual highwayman, he could return and hunt him down. Micah was youthful and inexperienced. Buck knew he'd have a minimum of trouble locating young Micah.

But the longer he delayed with the tangents that had so abruptly exploded around him, the farther away Lige Pheeters was getting with that stolen money. He knew what he *should* do, which was concentrate entirely upon locating Lige and the $15,000, but standing there above moaning Franklyn Connell under the steady, speculating black gaze of Tick, the Apache cowboy, he also knew what he would do. He would go after those murderous outlaws, try to keep them from killing Micah, and afterward try to hunt down Lige and the money.

If he failed to apprehend Lige Pheeters, he knew very well what Jim Evarts over in Lordsburg would say. He also had an idea what Cap Hanson would say—ask for Buck's resignation from the Arizona Rangers.

He kneeled down, shed his spurs, stood up, and said to Tick: "Get on your damned horse and lead out. I'll trot."

Tick stood adamantly shaking his head, making no move to obey. "You wouldn't last two miles," he said, curving his mouth into that raffish, cool smile he had. "You ride the horse. Remember, I told you how I used to run down antelope. I'll still be going when that Matador horse is ready to lie down and die."

Tick turned before Buck could utter another word, and started off toward the land swell where those horsemen had disappeared in a little shuffling jog that never increased and never decreased. He didn't once look back. His carbine, hanging at his right side in one mahogany fist, seemed to keep a kind of cadence as he ran on.

Buck went over, stepped up over leather, and reined out after the Apache. Off in the distant haze of the east red blazes of light were lengthening from a westerly, lowering sun.

They were nearly side-by-side by the time they approached that land swell. Tick was jogging along with his head down. The unmistakable tracks of the men they sought kept him thoroughly oriented. He paused where that land swell dwindled and let Buck go on ahead. Neither of them spoke and yet a kind of rapport existed. Buck knew what he was expected to do, and he did it. He rode gingerly around the sloping westerly haunch of land until he could see northward. There was no ambush. He twisted, flagged Tick onward, straightened back around, and kept on riding, northward now.

They left the land swell behind, pressed on with thickening shadows around them still following those tracks, until, more than an hour later, Tick drew to a halt, grounded his carbine, and leaned upon it, gazing thoughtfully ahead.

"Getting too dark to read sign," he said to Buck. "We've got to improvise."

"What?" asked Buck.

The Apache grinned. "Improvise. They teach you a lot of fine good English words at mission school. We got to forget their tracks for now and try to trail 'em by outguessing them."

Buck turned and considered the broken, empty landscape that Tick was so meditatively considering. "All right," he murmured. "You know the country. Where would they be heading?"

Tick had an answer ready, and a shrewdly observant one. "If it was they were just passing through like their kind often enough does in this desert country, I'd say they're making for the Dragoon Mountains. But that wouldn't be taking into consideration that they got Micah with 'em, and that they know about Lige and the lousy fifteen thousand dollars. So, my hunch is that they're going to hole up somewhere not too far off and get set to spend the night applying hot coals to the bottoms of Micah's bare feet to get him to lead 'em to Lige."

Buck agreed with this tough logic. The fact that he was convinced that Micah did not know where his brother was made it all the more imperative that he and Tick find those renegades. They'd kill Micah out of hand when they became convinced he couldn't help them.

Tick took up his carbine, cradled it in one arm, and said: "I wouldn't want to be in Micah's boots tonight." He stood a moment longer, looking out over the shadowy raw land. "We could wait until they light their supper fire, but that might be too late."

Buck leaned upon the saddle horn. In all that upended land ahead of them, running for miles and miles in all directions, a thousand men could have hidden themselves. "If we make a wrong guess," he said soberly, "we could ride right past them and. . . ."

"Yeah," muttered Tick, interrupting to put that one bitter word harshly into the stillness. He understood perfectly what Buck was thinking. If they didn't find Micah, and soon, they would never see him alive again. But something else was weighing heavily upon the Apache, too. Since Buck didn't know Perdition Range, the full responsibility of triumph or error rested squarely upon his own thick shoulders.

"You know," he mused, "when I was a kid in mission school, learning that life isn't really as simple as my paw and grandpaw said it was, I came to a conclusion. A private conclusion, you understand, because the mission Fathers wouldn't have liked it. I came to the conclusion, Buck, that the biggest sin in this life is failure. Not just murder or stealing or lying, but failure. Someday when we got more time I'll explain what I mean, but right now I'll put it this way. When a fellow does any of the mean things, it's because he's failed himself and has to cover up his failure by crime. If I fail to guess right this evening, I'll have to spend the rest of my life lying to myself and to everyone else to cover up the failure, and lying leads to other things."

Tick, while he had been speaking, had also been narrowly

studying that silent onward countryside. Now he started forward. "A man does his best," he said. "But it's not very often good enough. Come on, I'll do my best, and if I fail, my best won't have been good enough and no amount of justifying or lying will ever change that."

Buck went along beside the Apache, wondering, feeling unequal to his own thoughts concerning the wisdom of the pockmarked Apache cowboy. He was thinking that Tick would grow old with no more than he now had, a saddle, a six-gun, a battered old Winchester carbine, boots, spurs, and a worn old hat, and he would die an old man with his secret wisdom, without the race of men ever considering him as anything but a tamed wild man, a savage.

Once, as he jogged along at Buck's stirrup, Tick looked up and smiled. Buck smiled back. Something masculine passed from one of them to the other, something solid and unchanging. In this world of men they had silently exchanged kinship without thought of any differences lying between them, which seemed, there under the brightening stars in all that wasteland and great stillness, to be basically the essence of man's existence. What was required to dim out and shout down this elemental truth was town lights and crowds of dissimilar people. But here, there was nothing to impede the honest flow of their understanding of each other, and their respect.

They went along together, saying nothing. Buck wondered what Tick had in mind, which place out of all the dozens of sites hereabout he was making for. But he didn't ask. He was satisfied with the Apache's shrewdness and his integrity. As they passed along, he wished as much for Tick's sake as for Micah's, that the Apache would make the right guess.

Tick eventually jogged on ahead to lead Buck around the rim of an ancient meteor hole. He paused there to look downward, then went on again. Now, the country became more twisted and eroded. Oftentimes they passed through periods of near dark-ness where a sharply standing lift obscured the setting sun entirely. Once they startled a band of antelope and halted long enough to swear heartily at the dust those racing animals kicked up. But unless the men they were seeking were very close and watching, that interlude wouldn't be noticed because of the fail-ing daylight.

They had been moving ahead for nearly two full hours from the place where they'd left Franklyn Connell. Buck wondered whether Jennie had located Tom Douglas yet. He also wondered about Buster Pheeters in Connell's wagon, and he did not neglect to speculate on the probable whereabouts of Lige Pheeters.

He thought that Lige would be a long way off by now, squirmed a little in his saddle about this, and resolutely put it out of his mind. Lige would come later. When he thought this, he caught in his memory a very brief image of Jim Evarts's hotly indignant face back in Lordsburg.

Tick halted very suddenly up ahead. Buck scarcely had time to rein back. The Apache dropped to one knee and held that position without moving, without seeming even to breathe, for a full minute. Buck swung down, warned by Tick's rigidity that something ahead had captured his attention. He stepped to his horse's nose and lay a hand lightly upon the animal, ready in a flash to squeeze off any sound the horse might make.

"I think," said the Indian cowboy very quietly, "that we didn't fail after all." Without turning away from whatever it was that held his total attention, Tick said: "Look off to the left a little, about a mile ahead. That looks like a man sitting his horse next to some sage up there."

Buck looked and saw nothing. He was about to say so when Tick grunted deep down in a satisfied manner. "He moved. Keep looking and maybe he'll move again."

Buck stared and waited. When the movement came again, he spotted it at once because it was the only movement in that whole dead world ahead.

"It's a man, all right, and he's atop a horse. It'll be a sentry. But where are the others?"

Tick got up, eased backward until he'd put a jagged old broken ridge between himself and that far-ahead sentry, then motioned for Buck to get back out of sight, also.

"They'll be on that man's right or left. There are two narrow cañons up there. I thought they'd make for that place."

"Why?"

"Their horses would take them there. That's the only water anywhere around." Tick relaxed, swung to gaze at Buck, and made a mirthless, hard smile. "Those are seasoned renegades. They've learned how to get along in desert country. You look for water every place you go, but you really trust mostly to your horse's sense of smell to find it. Those men did that." Tick sighed and shook his head. He'd been under great pressure up to now. "That's what I was gambling on."

CHAPTER FOURTEEN

Daylight was nearly gone now. Those brilliant red splashes across the sky's underbelly were dimming out. Lower, in that vast tumbled world of Perdition Range, Tick and Buck lingered a while, letting dusk solidly settle around them. Only once did they step around where they might spy that mounted sentry again, then back again so he would not see them, and during this waiting time they discussed Lige Pheeters first, then the other things.

They were outnumbered and meant simply to utilize darkness as their equalizing ally, but, until darkness arrived, they slouched by that rough, broken old lip of land and talked.

"I think he made for one of the towns," said Tick, referring to Lige. "He's an odd man in some ways. Oh, he's plenty good with stock and ropes and the like . . . and guns, too, but the few times I've been around him, he's never seemed to me to like Perdition Range or cow ranching. He resents things. You know how some fellers are. They got chips on their shoulders. I don't know why, but they feel they got to fight or talk loud or cuss a lot. That's the way it is with Lige."

"And maybe act the bully?" suggested Buck.

"Yeah, he's a bully all right. I recollect one time we were making a gathering and a cut. He was repping for his family's cattle. Him and Micah. I don't know what started it, but those two tangled horns. It wasn't really much of a fight. Hell, Micah's not even twenty years old right now and this was a couple years back. Lige beat him pretty bad. Tom Douglas stepped in and broke it up. Ever since then Lige's had no use for Tom." Tick looked around at Buck. "He won't have any use for you either, after you licked him."

Buck shrugged. Lige Pheeters interested him only as the possessor of that stolen $15,000. "We'll meet again," he told Tick. "He'll get another chance."

But Tick said: "Naw, he's no match for you. You know that. So does Lige. So do I."

Buck looked around, and back again. "Who'd know him well enough to guess where he might go with that money?" he asked.

"I guess no one, Buck. Who'd know a man better'n his paw and his brother? No one. Yet those two rode all over the damned countryside today looking for him. They had no more idea than you or I had, where he'd go. But I'll still bet on Lordsburg or Tucson."

A horse cleared its nostrils far off. This snuffling sound carried easily down where those two were awaiting full dark, bringing their thoughts and their conversation back to the present.

"By now Tom and the boys'll be taking care of Connell and Pheeters," said the Apache cowboy. "And unless I miss my guess, they'll also be starting out after us, too. Tom's a rough man when he's roiled up. I just hope those yonder renegades aren't as rough."

Buck thought a moment, then said: "They will be, Tick. Their kind doesn't last long enough to cast a shadow unless they are tough." He gazed up at the sky. It was turning soft purple everywhere, but off in the scarlet west where springtime's crystal-clear atmosphere mirrored the final glory of the sunken sun beyond some darkly cut peaks and rims.

"It's dark enough now," he told Tick.

The Indian didn't move. He said: "Let 'em build their supper fire first." He was casual about this. "My paw used to say the easiest way to kill white men was to let them get hungry. They'd build a supper fire, then all you had to do was slip up and shoot them by their own damned firelight."

They waited a little longer, saying very little back and forth until Buck thought of lovely Jennie Connell and wondered aloud about her.

"Few women in this country," observed Tick. "Her maw died when she was a baby. Old Franklyn's a little like Buster Pheeters about womenfolks. I think in a way they're right, too. This isn't a good land for women unless they grew up here. You got to know how to live with loneliness or it kills you a little at a time."

"But Jennie doesn't know anything different, Tick."

"Jennie'll make it," said the Apache. "She's young but she'll make it all right. I think she'll maybe marry Micah, too, someday." Tick paused, craned his head around to see north-ward, and afterward qualified what he'd just said by adding to it: "If Micah gets out of this mess in one piece, I think she'll marry him. They ought to marry, anyway. If they don't, and if old Buster and old Franklyn go on picking at one another like they've been doing the last four, five years, I'd guess one of these days they'll have a feud going with one another."

Buck straightened up off the broken granite ledge, flexed stiff muscles, and stepped forth again to look up ahead. "There it is," he said quietly. "You were right, Tick. They've built a little fire."

The sullen, rusty glow of that fire beat upward from an ar-royo. It was a small, stingy fire so it didn't brighten the roundabout countryside much, but it did show upon the black night directly overhead. Tick, with his Winchester cradled, walked out, looked, and grunted.

"The question is . . . will they eat first or go to work on Micah first." He started forward. "Let's go find out."

They passed wraith-like through light and dark gloom,

sometimes skirting patches of thorny sage, sometimes skirting gravelly places that Tick seemed to sense before he stepped upon anything shifting that would grate in the night, and sometimes they halted to heed the hush.

Their progress was slow, necessarily so, but after a half hour they could hear men's voices indistinguishably and desultorily. They were by that time close to where they'd spied that mounted man. He was not still up there. Nevertheless, Buck put a hand lightly upon Tick's shoulder, leaned ahead, and whispered.

"Careful, they'll expect someone to try and find them. There'll be a sentry around here somewhere."

Tick nodded, shifted his carbine from the left hand to the right, and went onward very carefully, very silently, gliding in a typically knee-spring Apache fashion. Buck kept abreast of him until they came to a matting of dense underbrush near the rib of land that separated two narrow, fairly deep-cut little cañons. The right-hand cañon was where the firelight came from.

Tick dropped down upon one knee, held up a hand for Buck to do likewise, then leaned over to utter a few hushed words.

"We got to find the sentry first. After that, with luck, we can handle 'em easy."

Buck straightened back and dropped low enough to skyline the area for a human shape. He didn't find what he sought and it troubled him. The renegades down in their hide-out cañon did not bother him at all. Once he and Tick got rid of the elusive sentry, they had merely to slip up, poke their guns over the cañon's lip, and fire downward. But the key to this as well as the key to their entire venture and its success depended upon locating that sentinel.

Tick squirmed ahead into the brush thicket, remained in there for several minutes, then returned. His face and hands were scratched and his temper was showing.

"No luck," he growled. "But he's got to be around here somewhere."

They agreed to separate, to crawl off in different directions in their search, and to rendezvous at this same spot by going in a large circle that would end where it had begun.

Buck had crawled a considerable distance in his search when he was startled by the sound of a distant gunshot, pause, then another distant gunshot. He surmised at once what this was— Tom Douglas and the Matador riders coming up to help—but he did not believe that, if those unsuspecting riders had tried to select the worst possible moment to fire, they could not have picked a better time than this, when he and Tick were not only separated, but were in very real danger of discovery now, because, even as he had heard those gunshots, the outlaws would also hear them down in their hide-out cañon.

He reversed course and rose to go back the way he'd come in a darting, zigzagging rush, crouched far over except where underbrush made it possible for him to straighten up to look back and listen.

He suspected Tick would also be returning, so when he heard a noise off on his right in the middle distance, it did not at once cause him to do anything more defensive than swing around. He was moving like that when crimson muzzle blast lashed out at him. He felt the breath and the closeness of that bullet. If he hadn't been sideways, it would have struck him head-on; as it was, something tugged his shirt front. He dropped like a stone and rolled. There was no way now to avoid making noise because of the wiry, springy sagebrush limbs all around him.

That unseen gunman followed his progress with probing bullets. When he halted, he raised up recklessly and wrathfully and thumbed off two return shots, the hidden outlaw sentry also dropped flat. He also stopped firing.

Buck thought Tick had to be somewhere behind that sentry,

but he only had a moment to wonder about that. Men's alarmed voices rose up from that little cañon. Someone evidently flung dirt over the cooking fire because one moment it was brightly burning and the next moment it was not. Darkness replaced it with a black rush, absolute stillness came, and Buck got back down until only his eyes and the top of his head showed amid all that wiry, tangled, dark undergrowth. He thought the outlaws would be rushing silently up out of their cañon.

In the middle distance a coyote tongued. The echoes of this cry had no sooner died out than a second coyote tongued closer in. Buck thought that second call had been made by Tick. He noted the position and made a mental reservation not to fire in that general vicinity.

Someone said quite suddenly and uncomfortably close: "Fan out. They'll be comin' in from the south. Get 'em between fires."

Buck tried hard to locate the outlaw who'd said that but failed. While he was trying, the sentry called out to his companions, his voice muffled by undergrowth.

"There's one already up here. He's in that big thicket somewhere. I seen him runnin'."

Buck got down, turned, and continued his interrupted retreat. Someone back behind him, over near the cañon's crumbly lip, fired a Winchester. That smashing report was followed by the slashing sound of a lead slug passing through underbrush. Buck was tempted to fire back but didn't.

For a long moment there was nothing—no more shots, nor more calls. The night seemed ominously quiet. That overhead speckled sky was as serene as ever and a cocked-over, razor-thin moon rode indifferently across eternity.

Buck got back to his starting point. He searched right and left for Tick, found no sign of him, and thought the Apache was probably taking full advantage of the obvious fact that the renegades had fired at Buck and evidently thought he was the only foe they had this close.

Again those oncoming Matador men fired their signal shots—one explosion, a pause, then another explosion. Buck listened, considered replying the same way, did not because he knew the outlaws were gliding somewhere through the night toward him, and eased over into a particularly vigorous and spiny sage bush.

He was securely concealed, satisfied that the wisest course would be to await Matador, when off to the north a man suddenly gave a high howl and immediately four nearly simultaneous shots blasted the depthless hush, irrevocably shattering it.

Either Tick had jumped an outlaw or an outlaw had jumped the Apache. Buck held his breath for a second, awaiting some indication which of these things had happened. No more yells or shots came. He decided to go seek Tick. If the Matador cowboy was shot, he would need help.

Buck was leaving his sage bush, easing forward where milky moonlight showed into a tiny clearing, when another abrupt rash of shots erupted. This time he distinguished the unmistakable hard crack of a Winchester among the throatier, bellowing roar of six-guns. It crossed his mind that the outlaws, having located Tick off on their right and never having sighted Buck again, thought Tick was the same man their sentry had fired upon. If this was so, if the renegades still believed they were facing only one enemy, they might, and probably would, be concentrating entirely upon Tick.

As he eased out into that little clearing, he paused to look and listen. He had to know within a very few feet where the outlaws were concentrating and where Tick was hiding. In the dark, in all that sage, shooting at the wrong rustle of a man could cause Tick's death instead of an outlaw's death. But there was no sound. Once more that malevolent hush gripped the area.

Buck inched his way carefully northward. That firing had come from that direction, some hundred or so yards onward. He paused where it was safe to do so, still hoping for some telltale sound. Now there was nothing at all to be heard, which meant the maneuvering and counter-maneuvering was in progress. The outlaws were seeking Tick and the Apache was seeking to avoid being found.

Once more and for the last time, those oncoming Matador riders fired their signal shots. Gauging the sound, Buck estimated that help was no more than a mile back now, and also, estimating the earlier sound of gunshots, he deduced that big Tom Douglas was pushing up with all speed.

Someone else evidently had also gauged the closeness of those signal shots, for a man's voice boomed out wrathfully.

"Find him, dammit, an' hurry up. Them others are gainin'."

CHAPTER FIFTEEN

Buck placed the approximate location of that voice, corrected his course, and went toward it. He was certain, when he dared rise up, that the outlaw who'd given that sizzling order, was the leader of the band that had abducted young Micah Pheeters.

Someone on Buck's left got off one shot. It drew no response. For a little while there was silence. Buck used this respite to work his way deeper through a thicket, still heading for that one outlaw he'd located.

Two more shots rang out, both obviously fired by the same hand. Again there was no answer. Buck was beginning to think the same thing that bull-bassed outlaw evidently was also thinking.

The outlaw roared out: "He ain't firin' back! We must've drilled him. Head back for the horses an' let's get out of here. Them other ones'll be up right soon. Head for the horses."

Buck pushed aside sage branches, coming quietly up off the ground. He knew approximately where that man was. When he had his head above the brush, he raised his gun hand and waited.

But that renegade was, as Buck had surmised, an experienced one. He didn't stand up to push out of the brush; he kept down and crawled out. Buck could faintly see sage clumps quivering. He did not fire, however. He still wished to take no chances in hitting the wrong man. Far better, in his sight, to let one outlaw get away, than to kill a friend accidentally.

While he paused there in the ghostly half light with dripping night shadows all around him, he was torn between a wish to go after the outlaws, and seek Tick who, he thought, might have been injured. He went in search of the Apache, got down, backed out, and went around the sage clumps with more boldness than before. He had passed along nearly a hundred yards when he heard riders booting their beasts up out of the little cañon.

Once more frustration overcame him. He halted, raised up, hoping for at least one clean shot, but got none because the outlaws swept along northward upon the cañon's rim where they were shielded by sage.

He remained upright now. There was no longer much danger of being shot at by the fleeing men. Finally, with those hurrying hoof beats from the cañon diminishing northward, he called out. At once Tick replied.

"Over more to the west, Buck."

"You hurt?"

A thick shadow rose up and began shuffling around toward Buck. In a tone dripping disgust the Apache said: "No. They came close a time or two. My damned lousy pistol jammed."

When they came together, Tick held out his six-gun. Buck took the thing and examined it. The revolving cylinder that held the bullets had someway become jammed between two openings. The firing pin, when it fell, struck neither the right nor the left cartridge.

While Buck looked at the gun, Tick swore in both Spanish and English. "I couldn't fire back at 'em. They had my location figured out so I lay still. One of 'em got lucky and knocked off my hat with a slug, but when they heard Tom coming, they quit. That saved my bacon, because if I'd moved, they'd have plugged me sure, and if I hadn't moved, they were slipping up around me and it would've been only a matter of time."

Buck handed the Indian back his six-gun. Tick took the thing, swore at it, and heaved it as far as he could over into the brush patch. "Always did like carbines better anyway," he growled.

They returned to the broken ledge where the horse still stood, and made a smoke from Tick's makings. After they'd lit up, Tick cocked his head, listened a moment, then called out in a stentorian voice.

"Over here. Over by the claybank ledge."

Buck smoked and thought and waited for the Matador men to arrive, which was not a very long wait. He could no longer hear the renegades but the direction they had taken was fixed in his mind.

Four riders came walking ahead out of the night, one behind the other. The first rider was scar-faced Tom Douglas. He halted, looked down at the ragged, sweaty pair, standing there glumly smoking, gave his head one long wag, and dismounted.

"You boys've been right busy tonight," he drawled, stepping up to stand, hip-shot, gazing at Buck and the Apache.

"Jennie find you?" Buck asked.

"Yeah, she found us. We went first to the wagon. I left a man with Buster. Then we went over where Franklyn was and I left Jennie and another man. I sent another feller back for a wagon to move those two over to Connell's house. Then I started out to find you two."

Having delivered himself of this report, Douglas looked roundabout. "Where are they?"

"Gone," growled Tick, and waved an arm in a northward direction.

"Gone," echoed Tom Douglas, looking surprised. "Why, hell, there was enough gunfire going on up here to lay low an army."

Tick said a coarse word and added to it that his six-gun had jammed. Buck told the Matador men he'd feared he might hit Tick or even Micah Pheeters in error, so had not tried to engage the outlaws too closely.

Douglas considered this. He also seemed to be thinking distant thoughts, for a moment later he said: "Tick, where'd they go from here?"

"Toward the mountains, but they got a heap of hard riding before they get there." Tick looked at the men with Tom Douglas, singled out one man, and said: "Fred, how about you and me riding double?"

The cowboy called Fred said: "Sure. When we catch up to 'em, we'll borrow another horse."

Buck dropped his smoke, stepped on it, and waited for Douglas to speak. When the Matador range boss did not, but instead continued to stand easy and relaxed, running his bold gaze over the faintly lit broken land on ahead, Buck said: "The sooner we head out, the sooner we catch 'em and get Micah back alive."

Douglas turned toward his horse as though to mount. "I wouldn't bet a lot of money on that," he muttered, stepped up, and motioned for the others also to get astride.

The six of them, riding five horses, skirted brush patches between those two empty little cañons, broke out into open country, and rode along at a leisurely gait. Buck, feeling anxious and impatient, curbed his rising temper by rationalizing that the gait Douglas was taking was actually the best; they would have a long ride ahead of them. It probably would not terminate now until after sunup, and with one horse carrying double, a slow but steady gait was most likely to put them up with the fleeing outlaws.

There was a little conversation back and forth, mostly questions by the Matador riders that Buck or Tick replied to, concerning all that had happened before. Once, when the rider called Fred asked why Tick and Buck were pursuing the Pheeterses, an awkward silence fell. Tick looked over at Buck without opening his mouth and Buck, seeing Tom Douglas's gaze upon him, said he'd wanted to speak with Lige and would have let it go at that except now Tom Douglas spoke forth.

"I told you last night," he said to Buck, "not to start a damned war with the settlers. And you told me you wouldn't. You also told me you didn't have a grudge against Lige. That you weren't. . . ."

"All right!" exclaimed Buck, interrupting, satisfied now was perhaps the best time to bring everything out into the open since every one of those Matador riders was putting his life on the line in this fight. "All right, Tom. Micah Pheeters robbed a Great Western stage over near Lordsburg of fifteen thousand dollars."

Buck paused. Every one of those shadowy faces with the exception of Tick's turned aghast, turned utterly still and dumbfounded.

"He rode to Perdition Range with the money, hid it under the floor of his room at the Pheeters place. Lige found it and made a run out of the country with it. Tick and I tried to track him down. So did old Buster and young Micah. I think Micah must have confessed the whole thing to his paw. Anyway, we didn't find Lige, and meanwhile as we were heading for Buster and Micah, three renegades evidently passing through came onto Micah and Buster, somehow learned about the fifteen thousand after shooting Buster at the Connell wagon, or somewhere close to it. They took Micah with 'em, and that's about all of it."

For a full two minutes no one said anything. Tom Douglas kept staring hard at Buck. In a very quiet way he finally said: "And you . . . where do you fit in?"

Buck fished a little silvery badge from a pocket and held it out upon the palm of one hand. "Arizona Ranger," he said. "Captain Hanson's company working out of Tucson."

Someone let go a surprised swear word but Tom Douglas said nothing. He looked from the badge up to Buck's face and back down to the badge again. Then he suddenly laughed, bent over, and laughed some more.

"And Cuff had me almost convinced you were an outlaw," he said eventually, controlling his ironic amusement.

Buck grinned a little, pocketed his badge, explained how it had been that blustery night when Kennedy had seen him bringing in a manacled outlaw, then caught Tick's unwavering gaze, and shrugged at the Apache. It was now all out in the open.

The rider named Fred spoke up. "Tell me something, Ranger. Why are you chasing Micah and these owlhoots instead of chasing Lige and the fifteen thousand dollars? I've always heard Rangers don't never let up once they get on a man's trail."

"Maybe," said Buck shortly, "you've also heard Rangers are human beings. Micah's an outlaw for his part in the robbery, but more'n that, I'd like to see him alive so Jennie Connell doesn't get her heart broken."

"Yeah," mumbled Fred. "Only by the time Micah gets out of the Yuma prison, Jennie's likely to be old enough to chew iron and spit rust. *If* he gets out. From what I've heard of the Yuma hell hole, more prisoners die there than ever walk out again."

Buck said nothing to these observations but big Tom Douglas did. "Ease off, Fred. We don't have Micah yet. We don't have the fellers that're taking him along, either. As for the rest, suppose we just sort of hang and rattle. I think the Ranger here's doing right." Then Tom said something that brought Buck and Tick whipping upright. "If you hadn't given Lige that damned fresh horse when he came by this morning, the Ranger's fight would be over as soon as we catch up to these here renegades."

Buck was staring across at Tom Douglas who inclined his head ruefully. "That's right," he said. "Lige came to the remuda when Fred was rigging out a fresh animal. None of the rest of us was around. Lige said his own horse was going lame and did Fred figure I'd mind if Lige borrowed a fresh critter to head on home with. Fred gave him a horse."

Buck turned. Tick, too, stared bitterly at the cowboy called Fred. The cowboy made a wild gesture with his hands.

"Hell, I didn't know none of this. He acted natural enough. Didn't none of us know any of this until just a little while ago."

"Which way did he go," asked Buck, "and how good was that horse you gave him?"

"He went west in the direction of Tucson. The horse? Well, he was a big feather-legged critter with a Roman nose and little gimlet eyes. As far as I know there ain't no one ridden him yet. Cuff brought him up from the home ranch with other replacement horses a week or so back. I'd say he was tough enough and strong enough to get Lige to Tucson without no trouble at all."

Tick called Fred an uncomplimentary name. At once Fred began a loud, vehement protest. He reiterated what he'd already said about having no idea there was anything wrong.

While this harangue was in process, Buck and big Tom Douglas exchanged a solemn glance. Big Tom raised and lowered his shoulders. "He didn't mean any harm. It's happened before," Tom said quietly. "If we're afoot in settler country, we borrow a horse. It works both ways."

Buck said nothing. There was nothing to say. For once cow-country courtesy had backfired.

Tick, riding humped-up and grim-faced, turned back to studying the onward land. It was more broken, more brushy and forbidding the farther north they rode. What little night light showed was just ample to allow them to avoid the thing this entire wild and desolate upper reach of Perdition Range was particularly suited for—ambush.

It was Tick, easing on ahead with Fred, behind whom he was riding, who scouted the land for them. He knew the breaks, the drop-offs, and the sage-dotted intervening open places they crossed. The others had implicit faith in the Apache's ability to sense trouble; they rode along behind him, turning quiet. Even Fred had turned quiet, having run out of breath defending himself and his inadvertent actions earlier in that same day. He was glum-looking, though, not even the murky gloom could entirely hide that.

Tick eventually growled and Fred suddenly halted a hundred yards ahead. The Indian raised a burly arm to those behind; they also halted. Not a sound was made for the full minute this hush ran on. Somewhere far ahead the abrasive sharp scrape of a horseshoe grating over granite came mutedly down the night. Tick dropped his arm, slid to the ground, took his carbine, and, without a word or a backward glance, started gliding ahead.

Tom Douglas swung off, held his reins in his left hand, kept his right hand on his booted carbine, and said: "Don't make a sound, boys."

CHAPTER SIXTEEN

Tick was gone a long while. During his absence the waiting Matador men muttered a little back and forth, concentrated upon keeping their horses from fidgeting, and utilized this respite to rest a little.

Buck stepped over beside Tom Douglas. Those two kept listening to the onward stillness but evidently that rider up ahead, whoever he was, had been the last outlaw to cross some granite bed because no repetitious sound came back.

Buck said in a low, soft tone: "Tell me what you know about young Micah."

"Odd you asked. I was just thinking about him," answered the Matador's range boss. "I never cared a whole lot for old Buster nor Lige, but Micah was different. I guess maybe he was more like his maw than old Buster. If you're sure he robbed that stage, I can guess why he did it. 'Course, that doesn't change anything. An outlaw's an outlaw."

"Not always," murmured Buck. "I've run across my share of 'em. There are exceptions."

"Well, I don't know too much about 'em, myself," stated Tom, "but if there are exceptions, then I'd gamble on Micah being one. Buck, the beef market's shot all to hell. You know that Franklyn Connell's about to lose his ranch on a mortgage he figured to pay off this spring. Now that the bottom's dropped out of things, there's no hope for Franklyn hanging on."

Douglas turned his head to gaze steadily at Buck. He was

expressionless, but he was also appraising. He went on speaking.

"The kid would've known about that. He was in love, too. I'd say those are things that made him a highwayman. I'm not saying they're much justification. All I'm saying is that before a man judges or condemns, he ought also to understand."

"Yeah," agreed Buck quietly. "Maybe you and I look at things a little alike, Tom."

"What'll happen to the kid?"

"I can't say. You know that. It's up to Jim Evarts who runs the Lordsburg section of the stage line. It's also up to the law, and maybe to a lesser extent, it's also up to Micah."

"He's a good kid, Buck. Loyal as they come, hard working. It hasn't been easy for him. His paw doesn't want him hanging around Jennie. Her paw doesn't care for any of the Pheeterses too much."

"So I've gathered."

Tom was silent for a moment, long enough to listen to the onward night, to think a moment, then to say: "If it'd been Lige, I wouldn't have been so surprised. He's troublesome and he's mean. Old Buster's had trouble with him ever since Lige was a kid."

Buck put up a hand to silence Douglas. The pair of them, and the Matador riders behind them, turned silent, turned speculative in their dead-level onward appraisal of the night.

A moment more and Tick stepped up, grounded his carbine, and said to Buck: "They stopped up there near a spring to water their horses and take a smoke."

"You saw 'em?"

Tick nodded. "Micah's all right," he went on, "if that's what's bothering you. They got his arms tied behind him, but he was standing beside a horse like the others."

"What do you think, Tick?"

"We've got to get around 'em. This trailing 'em isn't going to do anything but maybe force 'em to fight. If we can get around 'em while they still think we're behind 'em, maybe none of us gets killed."

"Good enough," spoke up Tom Douglas. "You know the way, Tick?"

"I know it." Tick stepped away, went over to Fred, sprang up behind the cantle, and when the others all mounted, he murmured to Fred. Those two, riding double on the same animal as before, worked out and around to take the lead.

It was now past midnight. There was a distinct chill in the upcountry air and the moon, which had never been a great help, began to sink away and diminish its watery brightness.

As he rode along, Buck thought that, except for Tick's knowledge of Perdition Range, none of this would have been possible. He watched Fred and Tick on ahead, swinging steadily off toward the west. Around him the other Matador cowboys moved along as quietly as men possibly could.

For nearly a solid hour Tick navigated through this eroded land never taking a false trail, never once putting the party of them in any danger from broken, crumbly erosion banks. Once or twice he and Fred muttered back and forth but mostly they were as quiet as the others, Fred reining their burdened horse, Tick giving him whispered instructions.

Buck, who was entirely lost now, knew only when they began curving back eastward again. He surmised from this that the surrounding maneuver was now completed, that they were well above and around Micah's captors.

The air was a little warmer near the foothills, which was the only way any of them had of knowing that they were in fact close to the mountains. It was not possible to see anything more than a thousand yards off in any direction.

Tick stopped, motioned Buck and the others to come up,

leaned over, and said in a hoarse whisper that he was certain they were in line with the outlaws' route of flight, but to make doubly sure he would go ahead on foot and scout.

He did this, once more disappearing almost immediately into layers of endless night gloom. Once more, too, the others got down, stood to their horses' heads to stifle any sound the animals might make, and Tom Douglas was less than ten feet from Buck.

"This country," said Tom softly, "has been a badman's lair for more years than anyone knows. I used to wonder what the devil there was in a lousy desert that would draw men here. Hell, there's not enough water, the land's poor, the place is so lonely it weighs you down, and it's only fit to live in to run cattle and horses for three months in the springtime."

"Those," stated Buck knowledgeably, "are the precise reasons outlaws would like it. No one else wants it."

"I reckon so," mumbled Tom. "And, you know, ever since I can recall, there've been renegades in here, either passing through like this bunch or holing up somewhere like rabid wolves, waiting out some storm they caused somewhere else." Tom turned. "Now you know why I'm so touchy about the men I hire. In years past Matador's been used by a lot of outlaws for a place to be safe until some distant storm blows over. We've had shoot-outs between 'em while they were supposedly working our range. We've also had them raid the settlers, and one thing Matador *doesn't* need is bad relations with men like Buster Pheeters and Franklyn Connell. It's hard enough to get along with those men as it is, being that we all more or less use the same range, but with a few troublemaking dog-goned hiding-out renegades riding Matador horses, we could have real trouble."

"Sure," said Buck, understanding this as a kind of left-handed apology by Tom Douglas for having had his suspicions about

Buck himself. "Maybe someday things'll change."

"They'll change, Buck. Give the kid a chance and they'll change soon."

Buck looked surprised.

"What I mean is, Micah and Jennie. They're the kind Perdition Range needs. Decent folks who'll raise up decent kids. A few families like that with no more of the hatred and bitterness their paws have, and Perdition Range will change. Outlaws'll quit using the country for a hide-out. You can't hide out where decent folks got pride in themselves and in their land."

"You're saying Buster and Franklyn don't care about renegades being on Perdition Range?"

"They don't. Buck, those two old devils are like iron. They've been scratching in shallow earth for so long to build up ranches they don't give a damn about anything else . . . not outlaws they know damned well use their land to cross over and hide out in, nor the happiness of their girl and boy."

"You don't paint a very good picture of Buster and Franklyn, Tom."

Douglas went silent. He stood there, profiled to Buck, looking big and thoughtful and rough. Thinking back to their initial meeting, Buck thought how mistaken he had been about this big range rider with the scars and the iron-like, realistic logic.

Tom said: "Tick's coming back."

He was right. The Apache materialized as he'd done before out of the southward gloom, grounded his carbine, and leaned upon it.

"Heard 'em," he said shortly, "but didn't see 'em."

"Coming this way?" asked Tom Douglas.

"Straight toward us and they're riding easy, like men ride who figure they're in the clear. Maybe they sent a man down the back trail. If so, and he didn't catch any sound of us, they'd be acting relaxed like they sounded to me."

Buck spoke a name: "Micah . . . ?"

"Didn't see or hear him, but I counted their horses' hoofs and there are still four of 'em."

Buck turned toward Tom Douglas. "Let Tick take over now," he said. "He knows the country."

Douglas, gazing at the Apache cowboy, nodded and said nothing.

Tick made his little raffish smile. "Never been a boss before," he said, sought out Fred, and said: "The first thing we do is kill Fred for giving Lige that horse."

Fred's face broke into an expression identical to the one he'd used earlier in his protest, but before he could utter a word Buck warned him they could be heard if any of them spoke loudly, so Fred let all that pent-up breath out in one sizzling epithet at Tick. The men smiled, and Tick chuckled. He'd made his joke; it was over now.

"North of here a little ways is a boulder field. We'll walk up there, leading our horses, hide in the rocks, and when those fellows get in between us, we'll have 'em."

Buck liked the sound of this and said: "Lead out."

Tick did. Since he had no horse to lead, he swung along at a pace that made the others hasten. By the time the Matador men were in sight of the boulder field, they were breathing hard.

Here, in eons gone, some terrific upheaval below the earth's surface had heaved up enormous rocks. They lay scattered like tenpins in an area of perhaps ten acres. They were bleached to a consistent grayness by storms and centuries of summer heat. Most of them were much taller than mounted men and all of them were immensely broad and deep.

There was one central pathway among these huge stones. It showed faintly as a time-worn, dusty concourse over which wild game and Indians had traveled for centuries on end. There were other ways through the boulder field, but they were tortuously crooked, and unless one knew his way, some of them would lead a man or men into blind *cul-de-sacs*.

Tick let the others come up around him before pointing to his left and his right. "We'll split up. Three on one side, three on the other side. Now, listen. If there's shooting, which I think there likely will be, don't do like most white men do. Don't get them smack between you, and fire on 'em. Do like the Injuns used to do. Let 'em get on past a hundred feet, then shoot. That way won't any of us shoot the others because we'll all be shooting northward." Tick turned, looked into those pale, grim faces, waited for someone to speak, and when no one did, he said: "Buck, you and Tom and me'll take the east side. Let's go. They'll be along within the next half hour."

Hiding the horses was no problem. Among all those ageless big stones were innumerable little rocked-off places. After the men had taken care of this particular phase of their ambush, they filtered back down into positions among the boulders, three facing east, three facing west.

Tom Douglas, Buck, and Tick stood a moment together, harkening to the southward night. None of them heard anything, but Tick explained that by reporting that the land up to the boulder field was mostly deep black soil that would muffle sound. Then he said, as though this had been in his mind some little while: "Micah's lost his hat. You'll recognize him by that. I guess we want him alive, don't we?"

Douglas looked down and around. "What made you think otherwise?" he demanded.

Tick shrugged, looked southward down the corridor of the night, and said nothing for a while. When he finally spoke again, it was to avoid completely the former topic.

"Help like hell if we could catch one of their horses. My tailbone's getting sore from riding double."

"Hell," growled Tom Douglas, "Injuns rode bareback without

any pants even, in the old days."

"Sure did," agreed Tick dryly, with a secret wink at Buck, "but that's how you whites corrupted us. Nowadays an Injun gets blisters, even riding with pants on. You're making us weak and night blind and compassionate . . . which sure is degrading, Tom."

"Oh, go to hell," growled the range boss. "Let's get into our places."

CHAPTER SEVENTEEN

They heard the outlaws coming at the same time a very faint line of paleness firmed up far off on the eastern horizon. At first this promise of new day made no appreciable difference at all. The sky remained sooty; the world around that hushed boulder field was as still and ghostly and dark as night shadows could make it. But to Buck and perhaps to those of the others who noticed the predawn faint brightness it came as somewhat of shock and a surprise. Buck had long ago lost all track of time. In fact, if he'd been asked these past hours what time he'd thought it was, he'd have had to stop and think.

Now, though, there was only a moment to dwell upon coming dawn. Those oncoming horses were distinctly passing out of deep loam into the prefacing shale rock area immediately south of the boulder field.

Someone down there beyond sight mumbled something that sounded to Buck and the others like it might be a complaint or a protest. None of the other outlaws replied. The sounds became more recognizable as squeaking leather from unoiled saddles, jangling rein chains, and the small music of spur rowels broke the stillness.

The first outlaw firmed up into a solid dark silhouette as he appeared out of the southward night. The others came, too, with their prisoner, riding single file, looking tired and slouched and totally unsuspecting.

Buck's heart struck hard in its dark place. He kept low and

motionless as that first man rocked past. The second renegade was smaller than the first. Behind him came Micah, hatless as Tick had said he'd be, with his hands bound at the wrists and the short man in front leading his horse by its reins.

Behind Micah came the remaining man, a burly and bearded individual, looking villainous even in the dark. It was this one who said, just before that party passed far enough northward to be challenged by the hidden ambushers: "Reed, it'd have to be Tucson. I been pokin' along here, figurin'. He'd never try it over the desert toward Lordsburg. I say let's sashay over westerly toward the Tucson trace. We'll find him come daylight."

Evidently the man up front was named Reed, for he answered back, saying in a gravelly voice: "All right. We're too far north to cut around now and beat him to Lordsburg anyway, an' this ridin' toward the damned mountains isn't going to get us anything." This man paused, twisted around, and scowled back at Micah. "What d'you think, Pheeters? Would your brother head west for Tucson?"

"I already told you a dozen times," Micah mumbled, "I got no idea where he went. Paw and I couldn't find no trace of him."

"Yeah, but you 'uns rode east, you said, toward the desert."

"That's right."

From the column's rear the bearded big man said triumphantly: "That proves it, Reed. They looked an' couldn't find nothing, so he went west, not east, with that big fat fifteen thousand."

This one, being last in line, passed Buck as he was speaking. He was smiling. Buck rose up. On his right and left he glimpsed Tom Douglas and Tick also coming up from behind boulders.

Douglas bawled out: "Stop right where you are!"

A dozen things happened at once. The bearded man, closest to Buck, crumpled low and went for his gun. Buck saw him twist his astonished face as he did this. The man called Reed gave a tremendous bawl and hooked his horse hard. Gunfire flashed crimson in the night, bounced off gray boulders, and had its blinding effect upon men whose eyes hadn't been accustomed to brightness for many hours. Bullets and gun thunder crashed back and forth, making echoes among the boulders. Buck, concentrating upon that bearded man, heard his excited voice raised amid the bedlam, but didn't catch actual words. The bearded man jumped off his horse. It struck hard against the rump of the onward outlaw's animal and was stopped. Buck waited out two fierce muzzle blasts from that bearded outlaw, then thumbed off a shot. The bearded man wilted. Buck fired again. That time the big outlaw's horse jumped violently sideways as his former rider fell behind it, all loose and limp, struck down now into the dust and lying there, unmoving.

Swinging to the right with his gun, searching for another target, Buck saw that both Micah Pheeters and the smaller outlaw in front of him were gone. On ahead lay the man called Reed. His horse was lying across Reed's left leg, but the horse was serving his master as well in death as he had in life, because he made a solid, soft bulwark over which the renegade roared his vituperative defiance and shot back at his ambushers.

Buck saw Tick drop and thought the Apache had been hit until he saw Tick go scuttling northward among the boulders. In an instant he understood. Tick meant to get around behind Reed.

Tom Douglas roared out for the downed man to surrender. Reed answered by driving Tom to cover with a slug that shattered across a curving boulder near Tom, then went whistling off overhead.

It wasn't at all as Buck had imagined it would be. Somewhere off in the westerly night Micah and the outlaw who had escaped with him were getting farther and farther away while the

Matador men were unable to give chase because a pinned-down, fierce outlaw's dead horse blocked the trail with its carcass, and the horse's former rider kept anyone from showing himself with his wild gunfire.

Douglas called out again to that man, his voice knife-edged and deadly. "You shot out that gun, mister. Throw it away and give up."

As before, though, a bullet searched in the direction of Tom's voice, but this time the explosion was unmistakably made by a Winchester saddle carbine. Tom did not try to save the outlaw's life after that. Neither did any of the others. They fired into the dead horse, their slugs making a meaty sound as they struck.

Buck wondered were Tick was. It worried him because any of the bullets being hurled at Reed might go high and strike the Apache. He squatted low, shucked spent casings, and plugged fresh cartridges into his handgun. He had no carbine with him; it had been in its saddle boot when he'd given his horse to Jennie Connell.

A second of sudden respite came. Buck was turning when this occurred, wondering whether or not Reed had shot out his carbine. One six-gun roar went off somewhere beyond in the night, its deep bellow made doubly loud in the hush. That was the last shot. From out there where that solitary gunshot had come from a recognizable voice called irritably down the night.

"Hold it, dammit, hold it. You guys peppered the whole countryside up here shooting high. Now hold it!"

That was Tick. Buck faintly smiled at the audible indignation in Tick's order to cease firing.

"Tick," one of the westward Matador men cried out, "is he done for?"

"Yes. I got him from around here. Now put up your guns so I can get out of here. I'm cramped up behind a little boulder like a curled-up rattler, and you high-shooting idiots danged near gave me heart failure."

Buck stood up, stepped around into the open, and heard Tom Douglas chuckling as he also came forward. Together these two went forward to peer over the downed horse where Reed lay with his Winchester half across his upper body, his sightless eyes mirroring wetly the weak light in the sk̶y̶.

Buck stepped across, took up the dead man's carbine, and kept it. He started back for the horse from which the bearded man had leaped off.

Tick came forward with rock dust graying him, all but his annoyed, dark, and angry-looking face. He shot Tom Douglas a venomous look. He beat dust off with his hat, straightened up, and said: "You bunch of idiots. No wonder . . . hey, Fred, I bet that was you plastering my boulder."

Fred said nothing. Neither did anyone else as the lot of them followed Buck's example of going for their horses. But just before he turned away, Tom Douglas said half smiling, half serious: "You damned redskin. If you weren't such a tarnal disagreeable cuss, I'd give you a medal. Let's get out of here."

Tick came down from his lofty indignation as he went after the bearded renegade's horse. But as the lot of them rode around those two dead outlaws, he looked longest at the one called Reed and said with bitterness: "You got what you deserved, but for a while there I thought I'd be making the long trip with you, consarn it."

Tom Douglas was in the lead again. Buck was directly behind him. It was Buck who called out: "Tick, come on up here! Micah and that little one went west. Lead the way."

Tick jogged past all of them. As he was passing Buck, he said: "You heard what they said about Lige heading for Tucson. Right or wrong that's where that little one'll go with Micah. About now, with himself in the clear and his pardners dead, he'll be chortling, fifteen thousand dollars and all his now."

"Haw!" exclaimed Fred from behind Buck. "That little runt'll stand about as much chance facing down Lige Pheeters as the man in the moon. I say all we got to do now is trail him, slow and easy, and let Lige take care of him, then we take care of Lige."

Tick had an answer for that but Buck motioned him onward. "Take the lead and move out," he said to the Apache. He turned, saw Fred watching him, and gave his own opinion. "Lige won't be expecting any little stranger to know he's got that money, Fred. That little one can get right up beside him before he shoots Lige off his horse."

They were silent for a long time after this. Tick, riding ahead six hundred feet, was entirely visible. It didn't strike Buck right away that dawn was upon the land. The northward mountains emerged from shadows to stand immensely thick and towering, their squatting flanks dingy and barren, their upper reaches showing purple where firs and red-barked pines dwelt in crevices.

Ahead, well away from the boulder field, the land turned broken again. There were dense brush fields to be skirted, erosion gullies to be avoided, and, infrequently, little clearings where they could jog along, making good time.

It was colder as soon as they began drifting off southwesterly, away from the mountains. None of them had come prepared for this and they hunched along atop their horses like perching crows.

It was the dull gray time of day when nothing looked clean or pleasant or hospitable. Drowsing birds chirped complainingly as they went past, striking sage limbs with their feet, setting up a little quivering in the underbrush.

Tick maintained his leadership far ahead. He rode bent far over on the left side of his animal, looking disheveled and unkempt. He had not beaten off all that rock dust. He had not re-creased his hat either after he'd angrily crushed it atop his thick mane of coarse black hair. He looked more lusterless than ever, more like a venomous outlaw than either of those dead renegades back at the boulder field looked.

He was tracking Micah and Micah's captor, but it wasn't an easy accomplishment. There was just enough light to tantalize him and not quite enough to read the sign adequately. But he persevered. For a weary long hour he went along like that before halting, straightening up to rub his back gingerly, and mightily yawn as the others grouped up around him. He ran his tongue around inside his mouth and spat, and looked into those dusty, whiskery, gray-slack faces.

"You're sure an ugly looking bunch," he said pleasantly, all his earlier rancor quite gone now. "Look like a bunch of. . . ."

"Take a look at yourself," Fred broke in. "You look worse'n any of us."

Tick fixed Fred with his ebony gaze and broadly smiled. He drifted his gaze away from Fred and on ahead where the broken country was very slowly but gradually brightening. "Tucson," he pronounced. "And he knows the way, too. I've been wondering how fast he'll ride and how slow Lige was riding, and I don't think the renegade can get anywhere near before Lige gets to town. Lige's got too big a head start." Tick paused, swiveled his black stare around meaningfully to Fred, and went on in a rueful tone of voice. " 'Specially since Lige's got friends that set him atop a fresh horse and all."

Fred said something bitter and fierce but Tick only grinned at him. He stretched, dropped both thick, short arms, and took up his reins again.

"We'll sight Micah and his pardner within another few miles, I think, barring accidents. From here on the land's open enough. We'll soon run out of this broken country and get down where there's junipers and sage but not much of either. Then it'll become an endurance chase. It'll depend on who is wiliest and whose horse is strongest."

Tick struck off again, riding straight up for long intervals now, only occasionally glancing down at the tracks left by Micah's captor and his prisoner because he'd already traced out in his mind their route and, knowing the country as he did, he could satisfactorily surmise their course.

The morning steadily brightened along the earth's far curvings. Down upon that broad plain they were making for scruffy old ragged junipers appeared; here and there sage clumps also showed up. They left the broken country behind finally, and were riding over an immense flat prairie.

CHAPTER EIGHTEEN

Now that there was some light, without stopping, Tick raised an arm, pointing silently far ahead. Buck and the others strained to see that far away.

Two horsemen were heading west, looking very small and very close to one another. Fred hooted triumphantly but none of the others did; those two riders were a long three miles off.

Tom Douglas voiced an opinion that Buck shared. "We may get 'em boys, but it won't be before they reach Tucson unless there's some place around here where we can get fresh horses."

Tick shook his head as though anticipating the next and obvious question. "No ranches for ten miles. Not until we get near the outskirts of town."

"That," pronounced Buck fatalistically, "takes care of that, because they'll reach those ranches and get fresh animals long before we will."

They were quiet for a half hour after this, beginning to feel the despair that their bone-weariness made particularly acute, when Buck, keeping his somber gaze upon those tiny moving riders, suddenly drew up a little in his saddle, narrowed his gaze, and said: "Boys, something's going on up there."

Those two small figures seemed to blend, to break away, then to blend again.

"Fighting," opined Tick. "But I don't see how Micah can do much. . . ." His words trailed off. One of those onward horsemen suddenly veered off and went charging southward toward a thick, dark-looking patch of brush. Faintly coming back to the Matador men, so faint they scarcely heard it at all, was the far-away pop of a gun.

Buck looked ahead, then at the puzzled faces around him. He couldn't understand what was happening up there and just as obviously neither could any of his companions, not even Tick, whose eyesight was excellent.

That rider suddenly flung off his horse at the edge of the brush patch. The second man was left quite apart now. "If that's Micah," wondered Tom Douglas aloud, "why doesn't he high-tail it?"

Two more distant gunshots erupted. The dismounted man had faded out in the brush patch. Buck, becoming increasingly perplexed and troubled, spurred his tired horse. Without a word the others followed his example. All of them went careering swiftly toward those distant figures.

They were still a mile off when the bright sunlight jumped out of the east, flooding the land with its startling brilliance and warmth. It was this light that enabled Tick to see something that made him yank back hard and twist around.

"More of 'em!" he cried out. "More riders heading for that brush patch from the west."

Buck did not at once see these newcomers, but when he did, he also reined up. "Strung out!" he exclaimed.

Now the gunfire was clearer. They could not see anyone in the brush patch. Only the abandoned saddle horse remained out in the open, and that second rider atop his motionless animal a hundred yards beyond out in the open. Several of the newcomers spurred wildly for that second man. He made no ef-fort to flee.

Buck said: "That's Micah, that one sitting still out there."

Tom Douglas growled at Tick, and they all broke over into a lope again. While they were still hurrying along, a volley of shots came from either within the brush patch or upon the far, westerly side of it, where those freshly arrived horsemen were converging.

Buck tried to estimate the number of the newcomers but could not because of the dust down there and the constant movement. There were at least ten of them, though.

Buck was riding stirrup with Tick. Tom Douglas was back a few yards and the other Matador men were strung out around Tom, when, on ahead across the sage patch, a man's piercing cry rang out and almost at once several shots were thrown at the Matador men, now visible and coming on fast.

Buck palmed his handgun. He and Tick fired back at their attackers simultaneously. From behind them Tom Douglas yelled out that the range was too great for six-guns and let off a blast with his Winchester.

The men up ahead, suddenly seeing Buck's contingent racing at them, whipped around and raced for shelter in the brush. Someone down there was furiously yelling at the newcomers. Buck thought he recognized that voice but couldn't be certain until they were within a half mile and that discomfited man's angry roar continued.

He suddenly threw back his head and cried out his name. Tick swung to stare. So did Tom Douglas and the others. Buck ignored them to keep on yelling until that forward gunfire diminished, finally atrophied altogether. As he reined down to a slow jog and the others did likewise, still staring at him, he said: "That's Captain Hanson up there. Those must be Rangers with him. Hold your fire."

As abruptly as all that gunfire had erupted, it ceased. There wasn't a sound anywhere except the abrasive rub of leather over leather, as Buck and his Matador riders got up close enough to recognize hatless Micah Pheeters, sitting there, staring out of a gray face at them. On either side of Micah were two rough-looking armed men, who also kept an intent watch as the Matador men rode up.

A grizzled, older man pushed his horse on around the brush patch toward Buck. He had a Winchester carbine held one-handed across his lap. When he was close enough to make out faces, he said one sizzling word, upended his carbine, and dropped it into the saddle boot. He stopped, looked at the Matador men, at Buck, sighed audibly, and said: "Buck, dog-gone you, that was close."

It was Cap Hanson. Buck explained who the men with him were. Hanson nodded silently, looked for a long time at Tick, then jerked a thumb over his shoulder.

"Got a couple of dead men in there," he said, indicating the brush patch. "One of 'em a little runt called Beasley. He and two others shot up Lordsburg a week back. I got the wire they headed westerly out over the Pinals, made up a posse, and come this way. Darcy Mather's coming on from Lordsburg so's we could get 'em between us." Hanson dropped his hand, sighed again, and shook his head. "The other fellow in there, though, I don't know." Hanson's eyes went to Buck and stayed there. He said in a softer tone: "But I'd sure like to know how he came to be 'way out here on foot with fifteen thousand dollars in cash on him."

For a moment no one spoke. Buck dismounted. Around him his companions during this wild long ride also got down. They walked ahead where men had dragged two bodies out into the clean morning sunlight, placed them side-by-side, and stood back as the Matador men came up, looked, then relaxed, and gazed at one another.

Lige Pheeters was the larger of those two dead men.

Buck and Tom Douglas exchanged a glance. Buck was bewildered and showed it, but Tom wasn't. He said: "I think I know what happened. That gimlet-eyed, Roman-nosed horse

Fred gave Lige. . . ."

"What about him?" asked Buck.

Tom gazed at Fred, at Tick and the other cowboys. "No one wanted to ride him, Buck. No one'd try. He had the look and actions of a real outlaw." Douglas gazed over at Fred. "That's it, isn't it?" he asked the cowboy. "You never liked Lige any more'n the rest of us, Fred. You gave him that horse on purpose, didn't you?"

Fred looked embarrassed; he nodded his head up and down but said nothing.

"So," went on big Tom Douglas, "somewhere between the Matador camp and here, that horse piled Lige and he had to try and go the rest of the way on foot . . . with his fifteen thousand stolen dollars. That little renegade there, he spied Lige on foot. We saw him darting around down here after something. Lige ran into the brush patch. Those two shot it out."

Buck shrugged. He thought it probably hadn't happened exactly like that, but close enough. One thing he and the others were sure of because they'd seen it. Lige Pheeters and that little renegade named Beasley had shot it out in the brush patch.

Buck looked on out where Micah's captors were bringing him up. They had untied his hands. Micah rode right up and halted five feet from Lige. He got down without a word and stood there, looking big, and tousle-headed and somehow pathetic.

Cap Hanson came over, gazed briefly at Micah, then jerked his head at Buck. Those two walked out a little distance to be apart.

"That big dead one's the highwayman, isn't he?" Hanson asked.

Buck twisted to look back where Micah was standing. The others had shuffled away to leave the brothers alone for this little time. Micah's shoulders drooped, his raw wrists, badly swollen and purple, worked convulsively as the younger of the Pheeters brothers opened and closed his fists in anguish.

"Isn't he?" insisted Cap Hanson.

Buck turned back, avoided that question, and asked one of his own instead. "Was all the money there?"

Hanson nodded, keeping his hard blue gaze upon Buck.

"Will Evarts and Darcy Mather press charges if they get all the money back?" asked Buck.

Hanson said nothing for as long as it took him also to gaze over at Micah and back again. There was something vaguely like comprehension in the depths of his frosty wise old eyes.

"Why should they?" he said. "All Evarts wants is his damned fifteen thousand."

"And Sheriff Mather?"

Hanson made a grimace. "All Darcy ever wants is not to have to stir out of that office of his. Besides, who needs a dead outlaw when there's so many live ones around?"

Buck, watching Hanson closely, saw the hard, craggy smile forming down around Hanson's lips. "Tucson's a long way off, Buck. So is Lordsburg," murmured the Ranger captain. "In our files, which no one ever sees, it'll show that one Lige Pheeters was the highwayman who stopped lead with the loot on him."

Buck nodded. He started to turn back toward the others, but Cap Hanson halted him with words.

"Tell me one thing . . . why?"

"He's young and in love, Cap. He's not a bad man by any stretch of the imagination. I'm asking that he have this chance. He's just a kid."

Hanson put up a hand to stroke his chin. He looked over at Micah and said quietly: "But the man we were after is dead, Buck. I got no idea what you're talking about." Hanson dropped his hand, became briskly business-like again, and said in his normal, sharp, rough voice, "Where are the men who were with

146

Beasley? The leader's name is Reed. Where'd you boys leave 'em?"

"Back a few miles," Buck replied, also becoming business-like. "Send a couple of your boys back with the Matador men. They'll show where we left 'em."

Hanson said he would do that. He also asked Buck if he was going to return with the Rangers to Tucson, since the money had been recovered and the outlaws apprehended.

"Yeah," said Buck. "But first I want to talk to Micah and Tick and the others."

Hanson started briskly back toward his horse. "Be waiting," he said.

Buck went over, touched Micah's arm, and beckoned him away. As they walked quietly apart from the others, Buck said: "Micah, never tell anyone you robbed that stage. Not even Jennie or old Buster. No one at all. You understand?"

The bewildered youth halted, put his anguished gaze upon Buck, and stood there mutely. Buck faced him. They were less than four feet apart.

"Lige bought you another chance in life, Micah. He didn't mean to, and maybe he wouldn't have knowingly done it, but he's nevertheless done it. From here on it's up to you."

Micah's dull eyes moved a little, flickered with faint hope. "You mean . . . ?"

Buck pushed out his hand. "Shake," he said. "And when you see Jennie, tell her to keep that horse until I come for it, which will be the day of the wedding."

They shook. Micah's lips quivered; his eyes filled with hot tears. Buck dropped his hand, turned his back, and strolled over where Tick and Tom Douglas were talking with some of Cap Hanson's men. When those two saw Buck coming, they broke off and ambled out to meet him. Tick smiled.

"You'll be heading for Tucson, Hanson told us." Tick put out his hand. He and Buck shook. "Someday you come back through Perdition Range." Buck nodded, returning the Apache's smile. Tick turned, lost his smile, and growled up at big Tom Douglas: "Now I suppose I'll have to patrol that whole damned north range myself again. It took you two months last time to give me a riding pardner."

Tom looked somberly down at the smaller man. "Can't trust you," he mumbled. "Give you a pardner, Tick, and what do you do . . . land smack-dab in the middle of the damnedest fight you've ever been in." Tom finally made a whimsical little smile and looked over at Buck. "Good luck," he said. "And, Ranger, if you're ever around a Matador camp, just mention your name. From now on you'll be a legend among Matador riders."

Buck grinned briefly. He considered those two for a moment before saying: "Do me a personal favor, you two. Keep an eye on Micah."

Douglas nodded. "Figured to," he succinctly said. "Figured maybe to take old Buster and old Franklyn out behind the barn and have a real man-to-man talk with 'em, too."

Douglas shoved out his big hand. Buck shook it, dropped it, and turned when Cap Hanson called for the men returning to Tucson with him to mount up.

It was still early morning; the land lay brightly clean and scrubbed-looking in all directions. Far back where mountain haunches hunkered low, where a hushed boulder field lay, there was a quiet soft brightness coming down the mountainsides like golden water.

The new day was hardly warming up toward noon when all those different men separated, some riding westerly, some riding easterly, all of them riding with a sense of satisfaction in their hearts, but two of them in particular riding along with a re-affirmed faith in themselves and in their life's purpose.

ABOUT THE AUTHOR

Lauran Paine who, under his own name and various pseudonyms has written over a thousand books, was born in Duluth, Minnesota. His family moved to California when he was at a young age and his apprenticeship as a Western writer came about through the years he spent in the livestock trade, rodeos, and even motion pictures where he served as an extra because of his expert horsemanship in several films starring movie cowboy Johnny Mack Brown. In the late 1930s, Paine trapped wild horses in northern Arizona and even, for a time, worked as a professional farrier. Paine came to know the Old West through the eyes of many who had been born in the previous century, and he learned that Western life had been very different from the way it was portrayed on the screen. "I knew men who had killed other men," he later recalled. "But they were the exceptions. Prior to and during the Depression, people were just too busy eking out an existence to indulge in Saturday-night brawls." He served in the U.S. Navy in the Second World War and began writing for Western pulp magazines following his discharge. It is interesting to note that all of his earliest novels (written under his own name and the pseudonym Mark Carrel) were published in the British market and he soon had as strong a following in that country as in the United States. Paine's Western fiction is characterized by strong plots, authenticity, an apparently effortless ability to construct situation and character, and a preference for building his stories upon a solid foundation of historical fact. *Adobe Empire* (1956), one of his best early novels, is a fictionalized account of the last twenty years in the life of trader William Bent and, in an off-trail way, has a melancholy, bittersweet texture that is not easily forgotten. In later novels like *Cache Cañon* (Five Star Westerns, 1998) and *Halfmoon Ranch* (Five Star Westerns, 2007), now available in trade paperbacks from Amazon Publishing, he showed that the special magic and power of his stories and characters had only matured along with his basic themes of changing times, changing attitudes, learning from experience, respecting Nature, and the yearning for a simpler, more moderate way of life.